ZULEIKHA'S DREAM AND OTHER STORIES

Zuleikha's Dream
and Other Stories

Shamim Hamid

 The University Press Limited

The University Press Limited
Red Crescent Building
114 Motijheel C/A
G. P. O. Box 2611
Dhaka 1000
Bangladesh
Fax: (88 02) 9565443
E-mail: upl@bttb.net.bd

First published 2002

Cover design by Binoy Khisha

ISBN 984 05 1637 X

Published by Mohiuddin Ahmed, The University Press Limited, Red Crescent Building, 114 Motijheel C/A, Dhaka 1000, Bangladesh. This book has been set in Times New Roman. Designer: Babul Chandra Dhar. Printed at Elora Art Publicity, 635 North Shahjahanpur, Dhaka, Bangladesh.

Dedicated to
Ma and Baba

Contents

Preface

A large part of my professional life has been devoted to research on development issues, during which I have spent a considerable amount of time looking into the situation of women in Bangladesh and all over the world. I have found that if nothing else unifies the world, the strikingly similar plight faced by women everywhere, certainly ties all countries together. I will not qualify this by saying "especially the third world" because when you dig a little deeper, there is after all not as much a difference between the first and the third world as we might imagine — it is only at different levels and in different degrees.

In doing my research, I have consistently felt that I am preaching to the converted because what I write is read mainly by the development community — government, donors and NGOs — all of whom are officially mandated to bring about a change for the better. I feel professionally fulfilled when such a community is able to use my research for bringing about the desired change.

However, I have always believed that the message about women needs to be sent to a wider audience that does not read such academic treaties, but is certainly in a position to bring about changes in attitudes and behaviours that can help to improve the situation of women. True, I write in English, when the literate majority in my country read only Bangla. But I was not thinking of such readers as my audience. For them there are already the Bangla classics of Nazrul Islam, Rabindranath Tagore and Sharath Chandra, who were among the first to disclose the social double standards faced by women in our society.

I embarked on this journey of being a messenger to fill another niche. There is a new generation of educated men and women, boys and girls, who have grown up at home, imbibing traditional practices and attitudes, sometimes consciously and sometimes unconsciously. A similar generation has spent a major part of its life abroad. These young people are trying to balance multiple cultures and values, and in the process sometimes losing touch with the essence of their country — both the good and the bad.

It is my wish that these young minds read my stories and understand the underlying message that social injustice is pervasive and permeates all levels. It is my hope that they will use the knowledge and insight gained from the stories to realise that it is up to all of us to change attitudes and create an environment so that we can all spend our limited time in this world in peace and harmony.

It is said that a long march begins with a first step. My anthology of short stories is by no means a first step. Happily, many many steps have already been taken on the path to change. I am content if my stories induce a moment of reflection in my readers and set them on the long, long journey towards making the world a better place to live in. For then I will truly have attained eternal life.

Dhaka, August 2001   **Shamim Hamid**

ZULEIKHA'S DREAM

Zuleikha watched as her two-year-old son ran after her neighbour's chickens. He was naked but for a little round, brass bell tied round his waist with a length of black string, and a big black kohl spot on his left temple to ward off the evil eye. He was fair and healthy with large black eyes made even larger with black kohl which had smeared round his eyes when he had rubbed them sometime in play. His head was dark and shiny from the coconut oil which Zuleikha massaged into his thick shock of hair every day before his bath.

The day was hot and the leaves of the neem tree against which she leant were still and motionless. Rivulets of sweat trickled down between her breasts and she absentmindedly brushed away a tree ant climbing up her neck, attracted by the pungent odour of sweat. She was just back from the contractor's house. She went there daily to wash clothes and scrub pots blackened by cooking over wood fires.

Every morning, just as the sky began to lighten with the first hint of dawn, Zuleikha hurried to the contractor's house. The contractor was considered an important man in the village for he made lots of money organizing labour and material for people who built houses in the nearby towns. He owned vast amounts of land in the village and had built himself an imposing house in the colonial style with pillars and a long, arched verandah running the whole length of the house. At the end of the day, the contractor was fond of relaxing on the verandah, reclining in a long easy chair, and smoking his hookah or waterpipe, which his wife personally prepared for him every day.

The contractor was a rich man, and rich men have large households. There lived with him not only his wife and six children, but also his old father and invalid mother, his three younger brothers and one, as yet unmarried, sister. Besides the regular members, there were always guests perhaps from the capital, or from other villages, and sometimes even relatives who had migrated overseas and had come for a visit. And there were the usual poor kith and kin who did not have any fixed abode but spent a few months of the year with various well-to-do relatives, and so managed to keep body and soul together without having to do any serious work.

So there were always lots of pots and pans to be cleaned in the house. When she arrived early in the morning, Zuleikha would find the utensils waiting for her in the corner of the kitchen. She would load the greasy, smoke-blackened pots and pans into an old basket, and, balancing it on her hips, would call to her sleepy son to follow her to the pond. On the way she would stop in the courtyard to collect some ashes from the cold woodfire which had been used the night before to make molasses from cane sugar syrup.

The pond belonged to the contractor and lay a short distance from the house. The path to the pond was paved with brick steps leading down to the water's edge. The pond was an important source of water, for the large household did not have any running water system. Buckets of water were raised daily from the pond to fill giant earthen vats in the bathrooms used by the contractor's wife and his daughters. Care was taken to ensure that the water was clean but if sometimes a tadpole or two were found swimming in the water, no one really minded. But most of the others, including the contractor, used the pond for bathing and washing. It was large and deep, and the green waters were particularly inviting on hot days, so that even if he had the choice, the contractor was fond of saying, he would continue to bathe in the pond every day of his life.

Making sure that her son was playing in a safe place, Zuleikha would settle down on the steps to scour the heavy aluminum and copper pots. As she immersed the pots into the water, schools of tiny fish would shimmer up to eat the bits of dislodged food that drifted down into the water. She sometimes scooped up some of the silvery magic into the palm of her hand to show her son who would stare at them with large round eyes and try to grab them with his pudgy little fingers. But they were too quick for him, and Zuleikha would laughingly put the fish back into the water. She used a mix of ash and sand to get the grease, the spices and the soot off the pans. It was hard work scrubbing the big pots, but at the end of it the utensils shone like silver and burnished gold. Zuleikha was known for her ability to make pots shine and she was proud of her skill.

By the time she had finished cleaning the pots, the sun would be up and she would lay out the utensils in a sunny part of the courtyard where they would dry out in the hot sun and be ready for the day's cooking. It would now be time for breakfast and the cook would give Zuleikha a cup of tea sweetened with molasses and a piece of thick, round unleavened bread made from whole-wheat flour. Refreshed, she would suckle her son while gossiping with the cook and other servants. As the baby fell asleep she would lay him down on a mat in the corner of the large kitchen where someone was always there to keep an eye on him. She would then fetch the clothes that needed to be washed that day.

They would be waiting for her in a big pile in the corner of the verandah. A piece of lard-coloured soap cut from a whole ball, was usually lying on top of the pile. After she had done the washing, Zuleikha had to return to the contractor's wife whatever tiny bit of soap was left. The contractor might be rich but his wife ran the household on a tight leash. And with so many mouths to feed, who could really blame her?

Zuleikha would stuff the laundry into a large, aluminum bowl, and, balancing it on her hips, would once again make her way to the pond. The soap was strong and her hands would turn red as she pummeled the clothes against the brick steps of the pond. By the time she finished washing the clothes, she herself would be more wet than dry, but Zuleikha did not mind because she knew that the hot sun would soon dry her clothes.

Zuleikha carried the washed clothes, twisted like skeins of thread to squeeze out as much water as possible, to the rope strung between a mango and a jackfruit tree. She hung the clothes out to dry and if there were more than the rope could hold, she would spread out the smaller pieces on the lime and gardenia bushes dotted around the place. The dry clothes would be collected in the evening by another girl who came daily from the village to grind the spices and sweep and mop the floors of the many rooms of the big house. The contractor's wife liked to have many servants around the house because she felt that this way they did not get overtired and the large house was kept spick and span the way she liked it.

Besides, it only cost her husband the price of a meal for each maidservant, and as there was plenty of rice and vegetables from their many fields, the additional cost to the contractor was marginal. None of the women working in the contractor's house would dream of asking for wages because most of their menfolk were employed by the contractor either in his fields or in his construction work. This was an old, established system of patron-client relationship which no one really thought to question. Allowing their women to provide services for almost free was a way for the men to safeguard not only regular employment for themselves, but also to ensure that should the need arise, the contractor could be approached for loans for large expenses such as weddings, illness of family members or for replacement of sick or dead cows and goats.

That day Zuleikha was particularly tired because the contractor had new house guests and the washing and cleaning had been more than usual. She was late finishing her work and had just returned, bringing back with her her daily payment of a pile of boiled rice with a spoonful of lentil soup and some vegetable curry. Zuleikha knew that she had to stir herself to bathe and have her meal soon, because she had to be at the big house down by the river, in time for the old lady's afternoon rest.

The old lady was the mother of the present owner of the house. Her husband used to be the *zamindar* of the village, but, with the departure of the British Raj and the abolition of the old land ownership system, her son not only did not get to inherit the title, but also lost some of the landed property that had been in the family for generations. However, all systems have loopholes, and the family managed to hold on to a great deal of the land under various names. Unlike the contractor, however, this was old money. The villagers had special respect for this family and regarded the old lady's son as the Headman or village *matbar*.

Zuleikha liked the afternoons in the old house. She sat by the old lady massaging her feet with warm mustard oil and listened to stories about when the old lady's husband was a great landowner in the region. She also liked the old lady for letting her son sleep in the corner of the room on the cool floor. When occasionally the child stirred, she suckled him and he drifted back to sleep. The old lady did not mind these short interruptions in her massage. Her story-telling never faltered for she was talking more to herself than to an audience.

She liked to recall the days when her husband was the *zamindar* and she held so much power in the village. She and her husband would make regular visits to the capital to attend large parties thrown by the British Governor. They attended horse races and mingled with many important, white people at the race course. Now, no one in the capital paid any attention to deposed *zamindars* and life was not what it was when her husband was alive. Reminiscing in this way, the old lady's voice would drop to a whisper and she would fall asleep, snoring gently. Zuleikha would cover her up with the soft, thin quilt made from hand stitching together several layers of fine, old cotton saris. She would curl up on the floor next to her son until the old lady stirred and called for her afternoon cup of tea. Zuleikha was hired especially for the old lady and was not called upon to do any other work in the house.

Most of the old lady's grandchildren studied in schools and colleges in the capital or abroad, and came home only on holidays. But the old lady's son continued the lavish lifestyle of his *zamindar* father, so that there was always plenty of leftovers for Zuleikha to take home. So when evening came, and the old lady did not need her any more, Zuleikha would walk home balancing her son on her hips while carrying in her hand, an earthen bowl filled with rice, fish curry, and a generous helping of lentil soup.

The old lady often gave Zuleikha cast-off clothes for herself and her son. But at the end of Ramadan, on the great Eid festival, Zuleikha received her share of *zakat* and *fitr*, the mandatory almsgiving of rich Muslims. Zuleikha enjoyed these festivals because both the contractor's wife and the old lady gave her new clothes for herself and her son. On these occasions she helped in the kitchen to prepare the special meals for the feast days and was always given plenty to eat. If there were guests in the house they too would give her cash which she would ask the old lady to hoard for her until such a time as she would have need for it.

Leaning against the neem tree, Zuleikha was tired but happy. And at peace.

Two years ago her husband had gone to the city in search of a job. He never came back nor did he ever write to her. She was not surprised. Her son had been only a month old, and although she already had her two jobs, the payment she received filled the stomach of only one person. Besides she saw no reason why her husband would be anxious to return to her. She had neither looks nor money. With her dark skin and a squint in one eye, she could hardly be considered a beauty and by no stretch of imagination could she be considered wealthy. She had little choice but to accept early in life that she was ugly. Her mother, who was blessed with fair skin and brown eyes, had never failed to remind her of it daily, as if Zuleikha were to be blamed for being such an ugly daughter of a beautiful mother.

In fact Zuleikha had been so brainwashed about her shortcomings that she had been surprised that someone had even agreed to marry her at all. True, her husband was not good looking either, but then one could not expect too much when one had been oneself been shortchanged in that department. Her own beautiful son was a therefore a constant source of pleasure and wonder to her, and she felt that perhaps it was a way for Allah to redress old wrongs.

But Zuleikha found that ugliness, as well as poverty, had its advantages. Although she had been abandoned for two years, she had not been pestered by men to divorce her husband and marry them instead. She could walk about freely and safely and did not have to listen to sexual remarks by the village men. She was also left alone by her own family which was drowned in its own misery to be much concerned about her. Instead her father and brothers were grateful that she did not burden herself and her son on them. Her husband's family did not think she was their responsibility either. They insisted that as he was still alive it was only a matter of time before he would make his fortune and send her money. In the meantime she must manage on her own. Times were hard, and she must suffer like the rest.

Zuleikha, however, did not really mind being left to her own devices. For she had her dreams. Her own wants were so little that she did not even think about her own future. Her dreams were all for her son. She planned that as soon as her son was old enough, he should join the contractor's household or work in the big house by the river. Her son was smart and could have a lifetime's employment in any of these houses. In her old age Zuleikha would be able to live in her son's house and watch her grandchildren grow up around her. She did not doubt for a moment that her son would be taken care of, for it was customary for these two great houses to see to the welfare of the villagers.

The rest was up to Allah and the boy. From her own experience, Zuleikha was convinced that Allah took care of the faithful. Not that she said her prayers five times a day or fasted during the month of Ramadan for that matter. She was always too hungry after a full day's work to forego her midday meal. She did not, of course, confess this to either the old lady or to the contractor's wife because both would frown disapproval if they learnt of her lapses in following the teachings of the Holy Quran. But more than their disapproval, Zuleikha feared being deprived of the tasty tidbits that were prepared during the holy month of fasting. For they surely would not consider giving her any if they knew she was not fasting.

Blinking awake from her day dreams, Zuleikha yawned and stretched high above her head, the rough bark of the neem tree brushing against her arms. She stooped to pick up her son and was about to make her way to the village pond where she took her daily bath, when she was accosted by Anwara, her chicken-owning neighbour. Anwara was very excited. Yesterday some people from the capital had visited the village. A meeting had been held in the village marketplace, which had been attended by both the *matbar* and the contractor, so Zuleikha could imagine how important the occasion was. The visitors had spoken for a long time and although Anwara had not understood everything they said, she guessed that it was something profitable for the poor people in the village.

At the end of the meeting, she and a few other women had been asked to get together some poor women like themselves to form a group. These women would be given some sort of training and would be taught to write their names. Can you imagine, Zuleikha, being able to write your own name with pen and paper? After that they would be allowed to borrow money to start any small business they chose. They could buy papaya seedlings, grow trees and sell the fruit. They could buy some paddy, husk it and sell the rice. Or they could buy a cow and sell the milk. There were so many things they could do.

But Zuleikha was not interested in joining the group.

"What do I need money for?" she asked Anwara. "My stomach is full and my body is clothed. What do I know about business? Besides if I borrow money I will have to return it and that is too much of a headache."

But Anwara would not leave her alone. "Look," she persuaded Zuleikha, "You are working long hours for only two meals a day. You don't have any money. Don't you want your son to go to school and become a big man? Why do you want to remain dependent on other people all your life? With the money you borrow you can buy some chicken and sell the eggs and chicks or you can buy a goat and sell the kids and milk. You will not have to walk long distances to work, and you will be able to earn and save money staying right at home."

Something stirred in Zuleikha as she imagined her son as an important man who could read and write. Why, now only a few people in the village could do that. Besides the *matbar* and the contractor, the only ones in the village who could read and write were the village doctor, the deed writer and the old schoolmaster. The picture that Anwara had painted for the future of her beautiful little boy appealed immensely to Zuleikha. Perhaps she should not summarily dismiss Anwara's suggestions and should pay attention to what she was saying. Maybe there was benefit to be gained from these groups or whatever. Zuleikha agreed to talk about all this in more detail with Anwara after the evening call for prayers.

Three years had passed since that day. Zuleikha leaned her head against the neem tree, her back, bare between the blouse and the edge of the sari, felt the roughness of the bark. She was picking lice from her hair and squashing them between her thumb nails with a satisfying 'phut'. She had taken three loans in as many years and had every time paid back what she owed. She had a goat and some chickens and also had some money saved. Her son, still too young to go to the village school, was growing tall and strong.

Yet Zuleikha was not happy. Her husband had returned and the village elders, who had not been bothered about her survival when her husband had disappeared, now insisted that he was still her lord and master. If he had gone away for so many years it was only with the intention to seek a fortune for his family, they argued. And he did come back, didn't he? And it was not really his fault that there was no fortune to be made in town, was it? It is all in the hands of Allah, didn't she agree?

Zuleikha knew that it was her brother-in-law who had informed her husband about her new-found wealth. She did not begrudge using her earnings to feed the family but she did object to her hard-earned savings being wasted away. As soon as her husband had returned, he had sold her goat to raise capital for some vague business venture of which she saw no visible sign but smelt instead the rice toddy on his breath when he came home at night. She knew that he regularly gambled at the weekly market gatherings in the village common because Anwara's husband often saw him there when he went to sell his vegetables at the market.

Zuleikha also objected to the nightly sexual demands her husband made on her with her little son sleeping by her side. There was nowhere else that the boy could sleep. This was the only room in the little hut and even the goat and chickens shared it with them at night. That is, when she had the goat.

Since her husband's return, her finances were in jeopardy, and she could not save anything for her son's education. Her own dreams were being threatened. She was forced to default on her loan repayments, and, after she had missed three installments of her loan repayment, Zuleikha was expelled from the group and could not secure any new loans.

In desperation Zuleikha went to the contractor's wife for a loan, but fared no better. The contractor's wife did not want to loan her any money because Zuleikha was no longer working for them and there was no way that she could ensure that Zuleikha would repay her loan. And anyway, Zuleikha's husband was back and sooner or later he would find something to do and she would not starve. Besides, whatever happened to that wonderful women's group and the golden opportunities it held for Zuleikha?

Unable to convince the contractor's wife that she was not worried about starving but that she needed to save money for her son's education, Zuleikha dragged her tired body and mind to the house by the river. But the old lady had found someone else to massage her feet and listen to her tales of past glory. She was cocooned in her own world and really had no time for anyone, least of all for Zuleikha and her problems. She had almost forgotten who Zuleikha was.

No, Zuleikha was no longer at peace and she was no longer happy. She yearned for the days when life was simple and all her material needs were satisfied. She yearned for the time when she did not have to worry about saving money because her own, as well as her son's future was secure with the help of the rich families of the village even if her son could not read or write. She sighed when she thought about the days when she did not have to worry about whether her chickens lived or died or whether anyone stole her goat. She wanted to put back the clock to the time when she did not have any money, when her husband had abandoned her and when she did not have to submit to her husband's demands, both physical and financial.

No, she thought, having money created more problems than it solved. If she did not have any money her husband would not have come back to her and she would have been left in peace. Now her old jobs were gone and her husband demanded that she earn money or hand over her meager savings for his shady business deals. She wondered ruefully why she had ever let Anwara persuade her to change her life's course from that of a steady stream meandering peacefully towards a little pool to that of a turbulent river swollen by the monsoon rains seeking unknown paths and bearing away chunks of the safe and solid river bank.

As night fell and darkness enveloped the little village by the river, Zuleikha tried to push away the thoughts going through her mind and prepared for sleep. A moth fluttered around the naked flame of the kerosene-soaked wick of the little tin lamp. She unrolled her straw mat, fanning herself with the end of her sari because the small room was hot and the air outside heavy and humid. She lay down on the hard, mudpacked earthen floor next to her son who was deep in slumber, oblivious to the mosquitoes whining overhead. She partly unwound her sari, covered herself and her son with the end and settled down to sleep.

She did not extinguish the little lamp but moved it away from the sagging bamboo matting which served as the walls of the hut. She placed the lamp near the door which she had left slightly ajar to capture any elusive breath of wind in the still night. The lamp would serve as a beacon to her husband who had gone to the far end of the pond to relieve himself, taking with him the spouted container made from fired clay which they used for their ablutions. He had been drunk as usual, and Zuleikha had cautioned him about the slippery banks of the pond. It wasn't that her husband did not know the pond as well as she did, but he had come home swaying on his feet and it was more from habit, rather than from any real concern, that

Zuleikha had reminded him about the treacherous slopes leading to the water's edge.

Zuleikha scratched her arm where a mosquito had bitten her and yawned. Her husband had not yet returned but she could not keep awake any longer. Her eyelids drooped and she was drifting off to sleep when she thought she heard a faint noise in the distance. Drowsily awake and wondering if her husband needed anything, she sighed and got up to investigate. She wound her sari once more around herself and picked up the little lamp and went outside.

Peering in the dim light shed by the lamp which she carried more to avoid accidentally stepping on a snake out hunting for its meal, than to guide her along a path which she knew so well, Zuleikha made her way softly along the narrow path which was dry and mudpacked now but could turn into a quagmire of slush after only a brief rainfall. She could see no sign of her husband and walked to the end of the pond where she could hear low moaning. Holding the lamp aloft she could just make out the outline of her husband's body lying face down among the reeds and moss at the edge of the pond.

Her first instinct was to hurry down and pull him out of the water because shallow as the water was at the edge of the pond, Zuleikha knew that her husband had already lost consciousness and, if not pulled to the safety of higher ground, could easily drown in the few inches of water. Something however held her back. Her life in the recent past flickered in slow motion in front of her eyes. A drunken, out-of-work husband eating into her meager savings and earnings, destroying not only her peace of mind but all her hopes of seeing her dream come true about her beloved son. Zuleikha did not have any social leverage which she could use to divorce her husband, and he was in no hurry to leave her this time. For him the relative stability of life in the little hut, however dismal, was a better option than uncertainty and joblessness in the big city. And he couldn't have that if he did something as stupid as divorce Zuleikha, his golden-egg-laying goose.

The lamplight glittered in her eyes as Zuleikha made her decision. She tamped down the flame between her thumb and index finger and softly padded her way back through the dark, her bare feet making no sound on the path. Her coarse sari hugged her body tightly so that she moved like a shadow without the faintest of whispers. The water lapped quietly over her husband's face as a frog croaked lazily and glided across the pond looking for a better perch. The only witness was the *hootum pancha* on the branch of the jackfruit tree, watching sagely with its owl-round eyes.

Soon after, Zuleikha found that widowhood had remarkably improved her status in the village. The women felt sorry for her and decided to give her another chance and allowed her to join their group once more. She took out a new loan and bought chickens and a kid goat which she planned to rear in readiness for the Eid-ul-Azha festival when animals were sacrificed in commemoration of Prophet Abraham's supreme sacrifice. With only herself and her son to care for now, she had enough to eat and could again start saving for her son's education. And now that she was a widow, the village elders looked at her in a different light and even included her in some of the community activities. Zuleikha's day-to-day struggle for survival kept her too busy to be cynical about people's behaviour. She shrugged her shoulders and accepted the situation. If it made life a little easier she was grateful to Allah, and if it made it harder she took it as her karma.

Zuleikha was once more happy and contented. Her son was doing well in school and his future seemed bright. She doted on him and nothing was too good for him. She lived for him and dreamed of the time when he would earn a living, not by working in the fields or carrying headloads, but as an educated man writing with pen and paper. She dreamed how she would get him married to Anwara's youngest daughter, Amena, who was the prettiest of Anwara's three daughters. Zuleikha was already very fond of her, and Amena also seemed to have a special soft corner for Zuleikha and shyly came over to help her with her chores whenever she had the time. Nowadays Zuleikha seemed to tire easily and could not work as hard as she used to do.

As Amena rounded up the chickens for her, Zuleikha dreamed of sitting under the neem tree and chewing paan while her grandchildren ran around playing in the little yard which she took such great pains to keep smooth and free from cracks, by smearing it weekly with a mixture of clay and water. She dreamed of her granddaughter massaging her aching body with her soft hands while she told her stories about her father as a young boy. Zuleikha dreamed of dying peacefully in bed and being buried under the old neem tree that had been her companion for so many years. She saw candles being lit and incense sticks being burnt at her grave when Shab-e-Barat, the night for praying for all dead souls, came around each year.

Time passed and her son graduated from school. Zuleikha suggested that he begin work immediately as apprentice to the village deed writer or as supervisor to the contractor who had become old and feeble and needed trustworthy people to take care of his property and his business. Her son, however, had other plans. He wanted to go to the city for higher studies so that he could earn a good salary and take better care of his old mother. This pleased her very much and so Zuleikha continued to work hard and send money to her son in the city so that he could become a big man with an important job. And she continued to dream.

At first every week Zuleikha received long, two-page letters from her son describing the excitement of the big city, his college, his friends and the different people he met every day. She regularly visited the little post office and whenever she received one of his letters, she hurried over to the old schoolmaster who read it aloud to her. For although Zuleikha could sign her name in the bank books for her loans, she still could not read well, especially the handwritten letters which her son sent.

As the months passed however, the letters grew shorter and less frequent. They barely covered a sheet and were scrawled in such a hurry that even the schoolmaster had difficulty reading what he had written. Everyone in the village knew how Zuleikha lived only for her son and tried hard to console her. The schoolmaster, who had taught her son when he was a boy, explained to Zuleikha that higher studies in the city were not like village schools. Her son had to work very hard now and so could not find time to write letters. He would come home for Eid, the schoolmaster consoled Zuleikha, and then she would hear everything from him first hand. She would prepare mountains of rice cakes and *pithas* and cook all her son's favourite dishes. But she must not forget to invite her neighbours for the festivities while she was at it! teased the schoolmaster gently.

The rosy predictions, however, failed to materialize. The letters became fewer and far between. Her son moved from his old address and did not send his new one. At last his letters stopped coming altogether. Every time someone from the village went to the city, Zuleikha begged him to look for her son. They all came back with no definite news of him. Some reported that he had left the city, but no one knew where he had gone. Others reported that he had found a good job, had married the only daughter of his boss, and had moved to a new town....

Time passed.

Zuleikha stopped taking loans. Her own needs were so little that she could live on her savings now that she did not have to send money to her son. She had never worried about herself and did not intend to start now. Allah had always taken care of her, and she saw no reason why He would stop doing so now.

The *muezzin's* call to the evening prayers mingled with the faintly acrid smell of the neem leaves as Zuleikha hobbled over to the gnarled old tree and leaned her gray head against the rough bark. The eye with the squint had turned a cloudy gray and become blind with cataract. With her remaining good eye, Zuleikha peered down the winding path waiting for her son to come home. She had nothing else to do. She had no dreams.

THE HOLOCAUST

Hafiza cowered behind a tree in the muddy paddy field. It was a dark and moonless night and even the stars were hidden behind dense clouds. But she was afraid even to breathe in case the Pakistani soldiers raiding her village heard the ragged sounds of her fear-ridden gasps. She was terrified and bewildered because she did not know why all this was happening. She was thirteen years old, taller than all the other girls of her age in the village and with thick dark braids which swung down to her waist. She had large black eyes like her mother but her skin, while smooth to the touch, was very dark in colour. In a society where the standard of beauty was gauged by the lightness of the skin colour, Hafiza did not even come near to being considered a beauty.

The day had started normally for her when she had been awakened by the haunting strains of the summons to the dawn prayers. She had done her usual chores round the house, helping her mother with the cooking, cleaning and washing. When she had a little spare time, she had run with the old wicker basket to the nearby field to gather pats of cow dung which she and her mother would later make into dung cakes to use as cooking fuel. As she scooped up the moist little piles dotted all over the field, she had first heard and then glimpsed the young goatherd sitting under the shade of a tree playing his flute. She had blushed when, on catching sight of her, he had smiled and coaxed his bamboo flute into playing the hit love song from the latest movie. The song was being played regularly on all radio stations and was on the lips of everyone in the village, from the schoolboy whistling his way home to the rickshaw puller taking a break at the little tea stall.

Secretly pleased and flattered, Hafiza had returned home in a warm glow and later in the day, as dusk began to fall she had lit the little oil lamp and sat listening to her mother, Amena, reciting the Holy Quran by the flickering light, waiting for Hafiza's father, Altaf Mia, to come home. As soon as her father had returned, the family had taken their evening meal which was leftovers from lunch. Soon after everyone had turned in for the night, quickly dousing the lamps to save on the kerosene.

Her three young brothers had stretched out on a mat in the little raised verandah in front of the house, sharing between them two thin coverlets made from rags and lengths of old saris quilted together. Hafiza and her parents slept in the only room in the house. The bed, which occupied most of the room, was a wooden plank resting on four legs and the mattress covering it was worn thin and shabby. It had seen much use, for Hafiza and her three brothers had all been born on that bed. That night her father, tired after the day's work, had collapsed heavily on the bed which had creaked in protest. Her mother had climbed in after him and had as usual fanned him to sleep. Hafiza had rolled out the reed mat for herself on the floor, had unwound half her sari, and, covering her head and arms, had immediately fallen into deep asleep.

The village had barely settled down for the night when loud wailing and blood-curdling screams shattered the peace and quiet.

A light sleeper, Altaf Mia was instantly awake. Hurriedly fastening his *lungi* around his waist, he had rushed out bare chested, shouting to Hafiza and her mother, "Stay in the house and bolt the door. Someone is in trouble. Let me go and see if I can be of any help".

As they watched, Altaf Mia had rounded the bend in the path circling their little house and was lost to view. Her three brothers, excited that something was at last happening in their sleepy little village, tossed aside the quilted covers and rushed out after their father before Hafiza or her mother could stop them.

Hafiza had obediently bolted the flimsy wooden door while her mother took out the prayer mat and started to pray. Hafiza had joined her mother on the floor and had begun reciting verses from the Holy Quran. The screams had continued to rent the air and to block out the terrifying sounds, Hafiza had chanted the Quran louder and faster. Something was very, very wrong. And in time of trouble who else to turn to but Allah, the Merciful; Allah the All-knowing?

But even the solace from prayers and the Quran had begun to wane as minutes turned into hours and pre-dawn darkness had enveloped the village without any sign of Altaf Mia and his sons. Nor had there been any abating in the hideous screams. There had been sounds of gunfire from all sides but neither Amena nor her daughter had recognized them as such because they had never heard gunshots before. They could not even begin to guess what was happening. Extremely agitated Amena had hurriedly completed her prayers and folding up the prayer mat had said, "*Ma* Hafiza, I feel something is terribly wrong. The wrath of God appears to be on us. I must go and look for your father and brothers. You bolt the door and stay inside."

"Please Mother, please let me come with you," pleaded Hafiza, "I am terrified of being alone. I can't bear the screams and shouts any more."

"No, my daughter," said Amena, "It is very dangerous and your father will kill me if I let you out of the house. So stay inside, child, douse the light and keep very quiet. And pray for all of us."

So saying Amena had wound her sari tightly round herself making sure her head and body were modestly covered and had quietly crept out of the house. She waited until Hafiza had bolted the door behind her and then, swift as a shadow, went round the side of the house and into the screaming darkness.

As soon as her mother left, Hafiza had closed the Quran, kissed the book reverently, had wrapped it in its special cloth edged with silver lace and had placed the heavy book in its usual wooden folding stand. She had then blown out the lamp and, shivering with fear, had curled up like a fetus on her mat. All alone, she had become so frightened that she forgot even the Quranic verses she had learnt by rote. All she could remember was what every child was taught to declare before starting to recite the Quran. Whimpering and hiccuping, she kept repeating over and over again, "There is but one Allah and Mohammed is His Prophet, there is but one Allah and Mohammed is His Prophet, there is but one Allah and Mohammed is His Prophet ..."

Then suddenly, above the distant screams, came the sound of pounding feet, but this time near, very near. Hafiza shuddered, and the hair on her arms stood out rigidly in goosebumps. She peeped out of the window, taking care to remain out of sight. Disbelief flooded her as she saw her mother half stumble, half run towards the house. Her blouse had been ripped open in front and her breasts, firm and round in spite of breastfeeding four children, were heavily scratched and bleeding. Her sari was trailing behind her and the long petticoat underneath had split right up to her thighs. Blood dripped in a stream, leaving a crimson trail as she ran.

Amena had screamed, "Run Hafiza, run. All is lost. All is over for us." Then two burly khaki-clad soldiers had caught up with her.

Hafiza had been paralyzed with shock. In spite of living in only one room, Hafiza had never seen her mother naked and the sight transfixed her to the spot. She could not associate this terrible vision in front of her with the deeply religious and modest mother she had always known. She continued to watch as one of the soldiers dragged Amena by her long hair and the other ran his bayonet up between her legs. The soldier laughed and said, "Where do you think you are going, *haram zaadi*, you illegitimate bitch? We are not finished with you yet." Blood pounding in her ears, Hafiza heard her mother's agonized pleas, begging the soldiers to kill her.

Her mother's screams suddenly woke her from her stupor, and Hafiza climbed out of the back window and slid down the slope of the raised earth mound on which the house stood. In the cover of darkness, Hafiza had crawled her way into the paddy fields and had buried herself in the soft mud. Trying to quieten the loud hammering of her heart, Hafiza nearly fainted with fear as she heard rather than saw, two soldiers pass single file down the aisle between the plots. They stopped close to the tree behind which she crouched. But the *jawans* couldn't see Hafiza. Her dark skin had blended into the deep shadows of the moonless night.

"*Arey yar* , my friend," she heard one of the soldiers say as he lit a cigarette, "In Karachi we were told that the Bengalis in East Pakistan are all *kafirs* and infidels and must therefore be wiped out. But when we attacked that village, I saw prayer mats on the floor, Holy Qurans on tables, and also heard the *muezzin* delivering the *azzan*. What kind of infidels are they then, if they follow the same religion as ours?"

"You always were one to ask too many questions," replied the other. "Just follow orders. I am not bothered with who is an infidel and who is not. I just want to get out of this God-forsaken place which is covered with water, mud and mosquitoes everywhere you go. I remain hungry most of the time because no one knows how to make good *chapatti* and one cannot even get turnip here. These people eat only rice and fish. What I don't understand is why General Yahya Khan wants to hang on to this part of the country. Let these bloody people do what they want.

"Before coming here we were told that Bengalis only like to drink endless cups of tea, write poetry and discuss politics safely from their armchairs. That they are intellectuals and hate violence. That it would take us only a day to quell this stupid movement of theirs. But now I find that the Bengalis are small in size but are deadly in guerrilla warfare. I also hear that the Russians and the Indians are helping the Bengalis. In my book that, if nothing else, makes them infidels."

They quietly pulled on their cigarettes for a while, the red ends brightening and then dimming in the dark.

Breaking the silence, the first soldier countered, slowly and doubtfully, "I don't know. I don't feel quite right about the whole affair. Muslims are killing brother Muslims. Why can't the politicians fight this out among themselves? Why do we have to destroy villages and kill the innocent?"

"You are an innocent, my dear young friend," the second soldier had laughed condescendingly, stroking his thick, black moustache. He was very proud of his moustache because it was just like his grandfather's who had been a sepoy in the British army during the colonial times. "Those so-called innocent villagers of yours are really wicked devils. They feed the guerrilla fighters, provide them with sanctuary and act as their spies. We have to put the fear of Allah into them by killing the men and raping their women. Then the children born of our seeds will create a nation that is truly Islamic and in line with our own culture."

As an afterthought he had added, "But these bloody villagers are so poor. There is nothing to loot except a few gold ornaments here and there. I wish we had been assigned to towns, then maybe our pickings would have been a little decent. Look at what the idol-worshipping Hindu soldiers are doing in the name of helping the Bengalis. They are pillaging the houses of those who have fled to India for asylum. They are confiscating the Japanese refrigerators, video recorders and TVs because in India they are not allowed to import anything. These idiotic, *ullu-ke-pathay* Bengalis don't know when they had it made. And because of their stupidity we now have to leave our nice dry string beds to wade through these infernal paddy fields to teach them a lesson."

"Dawn is approaching," the first soldier observed, sadly shaking his head. "Let us return to the barracks. If there is anyone left in the village, they will be too maimed and wounded to be a threat to anyone for a long time."

The soldiers wandered away but Hafiza remained still as a statue, afraid that any movement would bring those *jawans* rushing back. She must have blacked out sometime during the long night for now as she opened her eyes, she found the sun beating down on her fiercely. The mud had caked around her and she lay embedded in the paddy field. She looked up into the sky which was already pale from the day's heat and listened to the keening and wailing rising and falling with the faint breeze blowing from the village. There was no tramping of soldiers' feet nor any more gunshots. Only desolate, inconsolable weeping — the living mourning the dead.

Covered in mud from head to toe, Hafiza raised herself on her hands and started to crawl to the edge of the paddy field. From there a sloping bank led to the road. She was about to drag herself up the slope when she felt a hand on her shoulder. She screamed in a voice she could not recognize as her own and felt hot water·trickle down between her legs. In her fright she had wet herself. Trembling in every limb, she turned to see an old mendicant peering into her face.

"Who are you, *Ma*?" he asked, addressing her in the common and affectionate term for daughters. "I thought that Yahya Khan's devils had killed everyone in the village except the old and the lame like myself."

"Old man, oh, old man," sobbed Hafiza, clinging to the old man's gnarled fingers. "What happened? Why were we attacked?" For she had understood little of what the soldiers had discussed since they had spoken in Urdu, a language she did not understand.

"Child, I am but an old beggar, illiterate and almost blind. I hobble from village to village and survive on what alms kind people give me. I know only what I hear from people on my travels. And this is what I learnt. You know that our country has two parts, West Pakistan and East Pakistan. We, the Bengalis, come from East Pakistan. But although we are more in number, and although a lot of the country's wealth comes from the jute which grows in our part of the country, yet all the power is in the west wing. We get little of the money or have any say in important matters of the country.

"Now we hear that fighting for the rights of the Bengalis is a man called Sheikh Mujibur Rahman who has earned for himself the title *Bango Bandhu*, the Friend of Bengal. He has the support of all the Bengalis and, in the recent elections, won most of the votes because there are many more Bengalis than there are West Pakistanis. But General Yahya Khan, who is now our President, refuses to make Sheikh Mujib the Prime Minister of the whole country. Yahya Khan has instead thrown Sheikh Mujib into jail and has sent his troops to our country to kill us all off. That in a nutshell is what this is all about."

Understanding very little of what the old man was telling her, and suddenly impatient to get home, Hafiza clambered up the side of the road saying, "I have to find my father, mother and brothers. I must go home."

Leaning on the branch of a tree which served him for a stick, the crippled beggar watched sadly as Hafiza, her mud-encrusted sari hampering her movements, ran awkwardly across the road and into her village. "*Ma*, be strong, and be prepared for the worst," he called to her. But Hafiza was already out of earshot, looking only towards returning to the way of life that she had always known, and the protection of her father and mother which they had always given and which she had always taken for granted.

As Hafiza neared her home everything was eerily still but for the sobs and weeping rising and falling like the ocean waves. She walked into the little courtyard of her house which she had swept and cleaned just last night before going to sleep. Even the broom stood in its usual corner where she had kept it after her work was done. Everything was the same and yet everything was horribly different. Her mother lay spread-eagled in the middle of the courtyard, naked and exposed with a hand flung over her eyes as if to shut out the horror she was helpless to avoid. Blood was encrusted all over her body in dark scabs. One of her breasts had been lopped off and even now blood was oozing out in a thin trickle.

Whimpering in fear and shock, Hafiza knelt down next to her mother and gently stroked her arm. Amena's eyes flickered open but they saw nothing because they had already glazed over. Hafiza quickly fetched the ragged quilts that still lay where her brothers had flung them in their haste and excitement to follow their father. She covered up her mother's shame and humiliation and, bringing out the Holy Quran from the house, started reciting from it. She started in a whisper and then her chanting grew louder and louder as if to push away the darkness that was stealing her mother from her.

It was thus that the old Imam from the village mosque found Hafiza, swaying back and forth and reciting the Quran as if to wash away the sins committed on her mother's body with the holy verses. Visibly distressed, the old Imam cried, "*Ma, Ma*, this is enough for now. Do not grieve. After what has happened to your mother it is better that she is with Allah than in this hell on earth. But tell me, daughter, what happened to you? Where were you when all this happened?"

Hafiza broke down at the sight of a familiar face for it was he who had taught her how to read the holy books and say her prayers. Sobbing she said, "Oh Imam Uncle, when the screams and shouts woke us up last night, my father and brothers immediately went out to see if anyone needed help. When several hours had passed and they had not returned, *Ma* went out to see what had happened to *Baba*, my father, and the boys. But she soon came running back pursued by some *jawans*. She screamed a warning to me to run away saying that *Quiamat*, the end of the world, is here and that we are all finished. Then the soldiers dragged her away by her hair and I jumped out of the back window. I lay hidden in the paddy fields all night and came back this morning to find my mother like this. Oh Imam Uncle, have you seen my brothers and my father? They never returned last night. Oh where are they?"

"*Ma*, by Allah's extreme mercy and kindness you were not found by these brutal *jawans*. Even if they had left you alive, your life would have been finished like your mother told you before she died. Had the soldiers had their way with you, your life would have become a living death, for you would have become a social outcast. That is the way it is in the village. But come, daughter, Allah has spared you the tribulations. Let us try to find out what has happened to your father and your brothers."

Her tears tracing little rivulets down her mud-splattered face, Hafiza followed the old Imam into the village square. People were gathered there in little groups. Women who had been raped were thrashing about on the ground, entreating Allah to strike them dead, for they had no homes to go to now. Hafiza ran here and there searching in the crowd and peering into faces.

"*Nani*, grandmother have you seen my father?" she asked an old woman sitting with her head in her hands. "*Bua*, sister, have you seen my brothers?" She asked a young woman with a baby suckling at her breast. But everyone looked at her blankly. No one had any answers.

Then, suddenly, silence fell over the people. The village *Matbar*, the headman, had arrived. He was fifty years old and looked striking with his well-oiled, white-streaked hair brushed back from the forehead. He was strong and vigorous and had inherited the headmanship from his father. He had had an able teacher in his father, and had learnt well how to manage the illiterate but canny villagers.

"Brothers and sisters," he addressed the grouped people, "It is God's will that I am alive today because it was only by mere chance that I had been called away to see a sick relative in town. Had I been here, I would have been the first to be murdered because there are those amongst us who informed the *shaitan* Pakistani soldiers who should be the first targets. The news of the holocaust in our village reached me early this morning, and I hurried home as fast as I could. I could not travel by open roads because soldiers are everywhere. I used all kinds of detours and that is why it took me longer than usual to get here. By some supreme mercy of Allah, my family had gone with me and was therefore spared. But my house has been ransacked and everything of value has been looted."

As he spoke, a few young and able-bodied men, who had managed to escape the massacre, crept back into the village, eyes darting here and there, unsure of their safety. The men were dirty and mud splattered. They had taken refuge wherever they could, on treetops, in ditches, and some had even submerged themselves in ponds. They were all strong swimmers, at home in a land crisscrossed with canals and torrential rivers.

If it crossed anyone's mind the coincidence of the *Matbar's* family escaping the holocaust, no one spoke up, at least not now.

"Brothers all," continued the *Matbar*, "those who are able to do so, please help me look for the missing people. Bring carts, rickshaws, any kind of transport, for the missing may be wounded and unable to walk. My own rickshaw vans are in readiness, but the bullock carts have to be hand pushed because the soldiers have taken away all the bulls, cows and goats. They have not spared even the ducks and chicken. There is no time to be lost, brothers, let us start right away."

His crisp white shirt and pajamas shining like a banner, the *Matbar* led the bedraggled group of people out of the square and into the only road leading to town. Looking for the missing was not very difficult. Whirlpools of vultures dotted the sky, and the stench of bodies rotting in the noonday sun pointed the way. A short distance along the road they found a mass grave. No one had bothered to cover it up and two pariah dogs were snarling over a dismembered hand.

Flailing their arms and shouting loudly, the men chased away the dogs. Then, one by one, they took out the bodies and laid them in rows. The lucky ones had been either shot or bayoneted to death and now lay with petrified eyes staring forever into the vast blue sky. Those less fortunate had been tortured to death. The village schoolteacher had his tongue ripped out because the soldiers were convinced that he had taught un-Islamic ways to the Bengali *kafirs*. The village doctor had his eyes gouged out for ministering to rebels and troublemakers.

The first to overcome the shock at seeing the terrible massacre, the Imam suggested that they continue their search for the remaining missing people. The old potter, whose son was among the dead, volunteered to stay back and keep watch. Hunger was overcoming any fear the dogs felt, and the vultures were slowly spiraling lower and lower.

The search party did not have to walk far when an overpowering stench once again led them to a pile of corpses thrown into a roadside ditch. The bodies were mutilated, sometimes beyond recognition. Stomachs had been ripped open and entrails were hanging out in bloodied ribbons Hafiza was deaf to the new waves of moaning and wails. She was looking at each new face being laid down and was hoping against hope that the rest of her family had survived the terrible night. But hope soon turned to despair as they pulled out Altaf Mia with his youngest son still clinging tightly to his chest. Altaf Mia had picked up the child and had turned to escape from the advancing soldiers when he had been shot from behind. Some *jawan* must have been very proud of his marksmanship for just one bullet had killed Altaf Mia and his baby son.

Oblivious to the stench and the myriad of flies, Hafiza continued to peer obsessively at the corpses. Near the bottom of the pile they found her other two brothers. Although nine and eleven years old, the boys had not yet been circumcised because Altaf Mia had wanted to make an occasion of it. He had been excitedly saving for months so that he could hold the ceremony in style for all three of his sons.

Thinking they were sons of Hindus who do not follow the Muslim custom of circumcising their males, the soldiers had cut off the boys' genitals and had stuffed them in their mouths before bayoneting them to death. The boys had choked to death, their eyes frozen open in shock and surprise. Next to her brothers, his flute still tucked into the waistband of his sarong, lay the young goatherd. He must have been killed in his sleep for he looked peaceful, and there was a faint smile on his lips.

Swatting at the flies and holding his handkerchief to his nose, the *Matbar* observed, "There are too many bodies and too few people to perform all the religious rites. Besides it is not possible to get at such short notice two yards of white unstitched cloth for each of the bodies. The heat is making them decay fast and we should bury them as quickly as possible. What do you suggest, *Maulvisaheb*?" he turned to the Imam.

The old Imam, nervous and shaken, had never faced such a situation. *Matbar Saheb* was right in saying that the burial should take place immediately. And it was also true that with the chaos that reigned in the village right now, it would be impossible to complete all the traditional rites. Besides, many of the living needed care and attention. So perhaps it was God's will that these massacred innocents would be deprived of even a proper burial, which is the ultimate entitlement of the rich and poor alike.

Shaking his white-capped head from side to side, the Imam said, "Let us take these bodies to the river bank and bury them together with the others in that big grave. We will hold a mass *janaza* prayer for the dead. May Allah forgive us the sins we must have committed, that we lived to witness this day."

The tired and exhausted villagers loaded the corpses into the rickshaws and handcarts, and pushed and dragged them to the riverbank. They returned to the village to collect Amena and a few others whose butchered bodies lay strewn about the village. The pile of bodies kept mounting. The vultures circled ever nearer. The pariah dogs squatted expectantly on their haunches. The *buzz* of the flies reached a crescendo. Sweating with heat and shock, the men climbed down to the water's edge to perform the ritual ablutions mandatory for saying any prayers.

The keening and the mourning had waned for the moment as the women watched from afar. They were barred by tradition from joining men at public prayers. The tattered group of men took their position behind the Imam to read the *janaza* and console themselves and their dead relatives and friends that they would all meet on the Day of Judgement.

Five days later, the ritual of *kulkhwani* was performed for all the dead. The *Matbar*, the richest man in the village, bore all the expenses of the rites which are usually held on the third, fifth or seventh day after death of a Muslim. It was the penultimate funeral ceremony. It started from early morning when the Imam of the mosque, his more able students from the madrasah, and some of the villagers recited all thirty chapters of the Quran as many times as possible. The reading was done rapidly and almost unintelligibly. Powerful prayers were repeated at great speed because the spiritual benefits for the dead souls multiplied cumulatively. The women could not participate in all the activities held in the mosque. They held their own gathering at the *Matbar's* house and, using dried chickpeas as counters, recited under their breaths the various prayers which were considered appropriate for the occasion. Later, all the peas were counted and the tally sent to the mosque to swell the number of times the prayers had been repeated for the souls of the dead.

The buzzing and the droning of the many voices ceased with the summons to the afternoon *Asr* prayers. Prayers over, the Imam gathered all the chickpea counters and calculated the number of times the Quran had been recited and the special prayers repeated. It was an impressive total. All that was now left to do was formally bless the dead. To do this a brief *milad* was held in praise of Mohammed the Prophet of Allah, who was then entreated to deliver the blessings on the souls of the dead. Once again the women could not join the men in the mosque. But the hymns and prayers were broadcast over loud speakers so that the women could follow everything from outside the mosque. At the end of the *milad*, at the behest of the Imam, everyone raised their hands towards heaven and invoked the blessings of Allah on the souls of the dead.

The ceremonies completed, the *Matbar's* helpers distributed packets of snacks among the villagers. The servants carried out wicker baskets filled with triangular cones made from dried leaves held together with slivers of coconut fronds. The cones held savoury *nimkis* flavoured with black cumin seeds, and fragrant balls of *laddu* made from gram flour and syrup. Most ate the food there and then, but others, too upset at the recent memories, took them home to eat later. The *Matbar* had been generous and had handed out extra packets to those whose family members had not been able to attend the ceremony.

Hafiza too was handed her share as she wandered about the square. She had stared at the cone and had then given it away to the old blind beggar who was tapping his way back from the mosque. Pleased at the windfall, the beggar squatted by the roadside and devoured the *nimki* and *laddu* with great relish.

Exactly forty days after the massacre, the *Matbar* performed the *Chalisha*, the final rites for the souls of the dead. The initial horror had already dissipated to some extent and, while people were still depressed, the atmosphere was less charged with bereavement and abject sorrow than at the *kulkhwani*. For this ceremony the *Matbar* had two castrated goats slaughtered and mounds of rice cooked. Reed mats were piled high with vegetables, spices and freshly butchered meat. The cooking was done over open fires and the air was redolent with the fragrance of curry. Dessert sat in rows of little earthen dishes filled with creamy *phirni* made from semolina cooked long and slow in sweetened milk flavoured with rose water. To break the monotony of the pale surface, one shiny sultana was placed precisely in the centre of each little dish.

Like the *kulkhwani*, the *chalisha* was also observed by holding a *milad*. This time it was held right after the evening prayers. As soon as the last blessings had been invoked for the peace of the dead souls, everyone sat down to sample what had been tantalizing their senses the whole day. Men and women sat in separate groups on the ground in the courtyard of the *Matbar's* house. Banana leaves, the precursor to modern day disposable plates, were placed in front of each person. The leaves had been cut from the plantation right behind the *Matbar's* house. Although the Pakistani soldiers had stripped them of fruit, the trees still stood with their large, flat, light green leaves whose oily surface made them ideal for use as plates.

Hafiza had been prodded and cajoled into washing herself and oiling her hair so that it now hung in shiny braids down her back. Her neighbours had dragged her to the ceremony to ensure that she had a square meal. For Hafiza spent her days roaming around the courtyard of her father's house, her hair uncombed and eating only if her neighbours took pity on her and left her a plate of rice and lentils. She now sat on the floor with the women and waited like the others to be served by the *Matbar's* helpers as was the custom.

The *Matbar*, of course, did not join the common people but sat in a chair with a few important guests on the verandah of his house. From here he and his guests could observe all that was going on. Special food had been prepared for these select few but they would eat only after the others had gone to avoid any ill feelings. Now they sat smoking and chatting on the verandah.

Keramat Ali was among the special guests. He was well known in the surrounding villages for his ability to arrange auspicious marriages. A lull in the conversation gave him the opportunity he had been looking for, and leaning forward he whispered into the *Matbar's* ear, "*Matbar Saheb*, do you remember you had once offered to buy that bamboo grove from Altaf Mia? He had refused because he had inherited the property from his father and wanted to pass it on to his sons. Do you remember?"

"Ah, yes, I remember. So what of it?" asked the *Matbar*.

"Well," said Keramat Ali, "Remember the old adage that a disaster for someone can be a joyous harvest time for another?" He wriggled in his chair, warming to the task at hand. "You know that Altaf Mia, his wife and his sons have all been killed by the *jawans*. There is only Hafiza left and by some miracle she has escaped being damaged by the West Pakistanis. I know she is very dark, but she is young and strong. I can show you the way to kill two birds with one stone. You may be her father's age, but by marrying her you will be performing the sacred act of giving an orphan shelter and protection. If at the same time you get the bamboo grove you have always coveted, then it is Allah's will. What do you think of my idea? If you agree, I can arrange for the Kazi to perform the marriage ceremony tomorrow. Actions should follow good intentions. There should be no delays, you know. See, there is Hafiza, in the third row."

The *Matbar* looked keenly at Hafiza who sat toying with her food. Yes, she was very dark, but she was also full breasted and exuding a sexuality which was all the more sensual because she was unaware of it. She was a bit thin perhaps, but nothing that a few good meals could not set right. She would make a welcome change to his second wife who had become fat and obese after bearing him only daughters. It looked as if Hafiza would bear him many healthy sons. And there was of course the bamboo grove - with a little bit of care it could bring in quite a decent income. Yes, Keramat Ali's idea was not bad at all.

The *Matbar* turned to Keramat Ali and smiled. "I always knew you were very bright, Keramat Ali, and now you have outdone yourself. I really need someone like you always by my side. Come to see me tomorrow and yes, bring the Kazi with you. Also send someone to prepare Hafiza for the wedding. She needs a good bath and some new clothes."

The next day some women from the *Matbar's* house came and dressed Hafiza in a new red cotton sari with a wide golden border. They accompanied her to the *Matbar's* house where the marriage was performed quietly and quickly. Hafiza's assent was taken for granted and there was no one from her side to demand her rights. Instead everyone was impressed at the *Matbar's* many kind deeds. He had not only paid for everyone's funeral expenses but had also given a home to an orphan girl. Did not the Prophet (peace be on him) say that taking care of an orphan was one of the most important duties of man? The *Matbar* really was remarkably good and kind. They would always make sure that he was the leader of their community.

That night Hafiza sat on the large four-poster bed waiting for the *Matbar* to come and consummate the marriage. As was customary, her veil was pulled down low over her head, her eyes cast modestly down as instructed by the women who had dressed her. In the next room someone had just turned on the radio, and Hafiza heard the plaintive strains of a flute playing the love song from the latest hit movie.

ROSHNI'S BABY

I am Roshni. Like most of the girls around here I am not very tall. I have very curly hair and velvety brown eyes which everyone says are my best feature. I don't know my age because my mother doesn't know which year I was born. But she does know that it was the year after the biggest cyclone that anyone can ever remember hit our little village of Borotara. Even my great grandmother, who I think has seen more things than anyone in the whole world, agrees that she has never seen anything like it before or since. The winds were so strong that the tin sheet which served as the roof of our house in the village was blown off, and my grandfather eventually found it ten miles away. He could identify it because he, like everyone else in the village, had put some special markings on it to prevent anyone from walking off with it when they were not at home. But my grandmother says that it was so twisted and warped that it was totally useless as a roof, and my grandfather had to sell a goat to pay for a new tin roofing. Anyway, according to the village schoolmaster, that would put my age to be about 18 years.

I do not remember Borotara at all. We had moved to the city while I was still an infant because my father had a job as a gardener in a rich man's house. We lived in a room in the servants' quarters, and I recall helping my father collect dead leaves and twigs from the smooth green lawn in front of the house. We did not stay in that house very long because my father got tuberculosis and soon became too weak to work. His employer, the rich man, was kind and paid his hospital costs, but it was too late, and my father died soon after he had been admitted into the hospital.

My father's employer already had several servants and did not need another one but he helped my mother find a job as a maidservant in another house. The people, however, did not want my mother to live-in as they did not want to have a small child running around the place. So my mother asked around and eventually found a shack in a slum which spreads out over quite a large area alongside this great big road which leads to the airport. Once in a while the Government sends van loads of policemen with a bulldozer to break down our shacks and move us out of the place because we are an eyesore, especially when important people from abroad come to visit our country. But the police do their job halfheartedly because they know and we know that, as soon as they have gone, we will again build up our shacks. It does not take very long to put up four matted-bamboo walls and throw over a sheet of plastic for a roof. All those who live in the slum have nowhere else to go, so we are not going to move from this place in a hurry. Besides, once in a while, some people come to us and tell us that they are lawyers and human rights activists, whatever that means. But we are always happy to talk to them because they are helpful and they encourage us to stay in the slum saying that the Government can force us to move out only if it provides us with some other place to stay. These activists even convinced some of the slum dwellers to sue the Government, and we were told that some very important lawyers would take the case to court.

My mother is not interested in any of this and only wants to be left alone to lead her own life. Our house consists of one small room with a tiny kerosene stove in a corner which serves as a kitchen. We use the stove sparingly as oil is very expensive. There are two tubewells for drinking water which have been installed by an organization that is trying to set up a school for the children in the area. They have not as yet been very successful in getting the children to attend classes because even four- and five-year-olds go out to collect scrap paper, used tins and broken bottles from streets and dustbins. These can fetch quite a good price when sold to the ragman who comes around once a week to our slum. So it is foolish of the people from the organization to think that anyone would send their children to school when they can earn money which the family needs so badly.

I myself have never been to school. I have been a servant girl ever since I can remember. Even as a little girl I walked every day with my mother to the big white house in that part of town where the rich live. My mother worked there as a charwoman and every day she scrubbed the pots and pans, washed clothes and wiped the floor on her hands and knees. My mother liked swabbing the smooth, cool floor and, after she finished cleaning it, the red floor gleamed with a life of its own. You could almost see your face reflected in it.

Although I was only five years old then, I too had to earn my keep as my mother received food rations for both of us. While my mother went about her chores, I was put to minding the new baby. My duty was to chase away any flies and mosquitoes that might bother him while he slept. If he woke up before his milk time then I would gently rock his cradle till he fell asleep again. If he was stubborn and refused to go back to sleep, I went and fetched his mother for I had strict instructions that on no occasion was I to try and take the baby in my lap when I was alone because I was too young. The baby's mother was the lady of the house and my mother addressed her as *Apa*, Big Sister, because she was too young to be called *Amma* (Mother) or *Khalamma* (Aunty), by my mother. That relationship established the Mistress as my mother's sister, so naturally I called her Aunty.

When I was not minding the baby, I did little chores around the house such as fetching this and that, calling the cook when Aunty wanted to talk to him, running upstairs to carry the newspapers to *Dadima*, who was the Master's mother and lived in the same house with them. My mother and I stayed in the house the whole day and were given morning breakfast of unleavened bread and tea. Lunch consisted of rice, lentils and vegetables and sometimes fish curry, and, just before we left in the evening, we were given tea and biscuits. Aunty and the Master were very good to us and as I grew up I saw their family grow from just one baby son to three sons and two daughters.

But by this time I too had grown up and my mother found me another house to work in, where, besides meals, I would also receive some wages. My new Master was a government servant and not as rich as the businessman who employed my mother. The agreement between my mother and my new Master was that I would get monthly wages and two meals a day. But the Mistress, whom I again addressed as Aunty, was forever locking up everything in the kitchen as if she was afraid that when her back was turned I would eat everything in her fridge and storeroom. Because of this, I had to sometimes do without my tea, because she would have been away the whole afternoon and by the time she returned home, I would have to leave because I always liked to get home before dark.

My new Aunty was not as nice as the old one. She was very ill-tempered and never satisfied with my work. But I suspected that she made that an excuse for giving me less to eat. She was forever reducing my portion of rice, saying that she could not give me a full meal if I did not do a full day's work. She also held on to my pay for months on end, saying that she was saving it for me as otherwise I would go and waste it on rubbish and nonsense. So every few months my mother had to come and cajole, beg and wheedle my wages out of Aunty.

Other things were also beginning to happen. I was growing up fast, and when the Master was home, I found him glancing at me with a certain look in his eye. Whenever he got the chance, he would touch my hands or squeeze my shoulders. I told my mother about the Master, but all she said was that such things happen, and that I should not make too much of a fuss about it. She said that we badly needed the job, and all I had to do was make sure that I never remained alone with the Master for too long. One day, however, Aunty caught the Master caressing my hair and face, and the very next day she called my mother, gave her my full wages and told her that she did not want me to work for her anymore.

It was not very difficult for me to find another job because nowadays all young girls from the village want to work in garment factories and it is hard to find domestic help. So I got this new job where, like my mother, I cleaned pots and pans, washed clothes, and wiped the floor. There were no other servants in the house and I lived in with the family. I managed the work because the apartment was small and the family consisted of only the Master and the Mistress whose children lived and worked overseas. My employers were elderly people and, as is the custom in such cases, I addressed them as Father and Mother.

One day, as I walked downstairs to take out the garbage, I met Abdul who worked as a cook in the apartment next door. He was very good looking, with teasing black eyes and a flashing white smile. We stood chatting by the pile of rubbish in the corner of the road where everyone dumped their garbage. Flies buzzed all around, and the air was ripe with the smell of rotting food. But I barely noticed any of this. Abdul's eyes bored into mine, and I was so flattered by all the attention that if the house was on fire, I would not have known it.

Soon, however, I had to reluctantly take leave of Abdul, as it was getting late, and my Mistress would be wondering where I had disappeared. I turned to go, but Abdul caught my hand and said that he wanted to see me again soon, very soon. That if I took a day off from work, he would take me into town to eat in a restaurant and to see a movie. I had never been to the movies before because they cost too much. The only movies I ever saw were old ones shown on the television which my Mistress sometimes turned on in the evenings. She said the programmes were very boring and she preferred to read a book or write letters to her children.

The next day I asked for a day off, making the excuse that I wanted to go and see my mother who was not feeling too well. Since I seldom took any holidays, my Mistress was quite willing to give me time off. I took special care to dress nicely and put on the new red and green cotton sari that the Mistress had given me last Eid. I had arranged with Abdul to meet him at the bus stop because I did not want my

Mistress to know that I was going out with the next-door cook. My Mistress is very old-fashioned and does not like me getting friendly with men.

I found Abdul waiting for me under the shade of a tree, smoking a cigarette. The way he looked me up and down made me feel very beautiful and desirable. I suddenly felt very shy, but at the same time all warm and squishy inside. We did not have to wait long for the bus which took us straight into the old part of town. It is always very exciting here. The streets are crowded with cars and rickshaws which move so slowly that one can weave one's way through the traffic without any fear of being run over. Little shops line the narrow streets and one can buy anything imaginable in these stalls — from gold jewelry to iron rods, from wooden planks to beautiful, hand-crafted silver plates and dishes.

Abdul took me to a wayside food stall where we ate steaming *biryani* made from fragrant rice and castrated goat meat. Dessert consisted of dollops of saffron-coloured yogurt, spooned out from large earthenware bowls. We ended our meal with cups of strong tea and sweet paan stuffed with herbs and shredded coconut dyed red and yellow. Satiated, we went to see a movie where the heroine was poor but very beautiful and the hero, the only son of a very rich landowner. The hero had espied the heroine taking a bath in the village pond and had promptly fallen so deeply in love with her that, when some dacoits raided the village and carried her off as part of the booty, the hero rose to the occasion, and single-handedly fought a dozen bandits to save the heroine from a fate worse than death.

It was all very romantic so that on the way home, when Abdul started kissing me in the rickshaw, I was only too happy to fall into his arms. He was not the only son of a rich landowner, but, for the time being, he would have to do. We went to Ramna Park which is very famous for its many varieties of trees and bushes. Once on the way to the market, as we were passing by the park, my Mistress told me that it had been established by an Englishman some seventy years ago and has a good collection of unusual plants and shrubs.

At sundown, however, the park is avoided by most people except couples like us. Twilight had fallen by the time the rickshaw set us down at the park's main gate. The sky had turned a deep purple and you could barely make out the dark shapes behind bushes and shrubs. Abdul chose a large bush studded with bright yellow, trumpet-shaped flowers and, in its dusky shadows, he made love to me, first gently, then with more and more frenzy. I did not particularly enjoy it because it hurt quite a bit, but I was ecstatic that someone could love me and want me as much as Abdul did.

A few weeks after that very exciting day, I started to feel dizzy in the mornings and too nauseated to take breakfast. At first my Mistress thought that I was coming down with jaundice. But when she found that I did not have any fever, and that later in the day I displayed my usual healthy appetite, she asked me if I had missed any of my periods. I admitted that I had, and she looked at me very sternly and told me that she did not know how this could have happened, seeing that she had always kept a close eye on me. She took me to see a doctor who confirmed that I was indeed pregnant. My Mistress then told me that, much as she liked me and my work, it was not possible for her to employ me anymore.

So I went home to our little shack in the slum and told my mother that my employers had gone abroad for a few months and had told me to go back when they returned. I also told my mother that I would find another job to do during this time but that I wanted to rest for a few days as I was very tired. My mother never suspected anything because she left early in the morning before I woke up, and so did not see any of my morning sickness. Within a few weeks I started feeling fine and managed to find myself a new job.

In my new place of work I, of course, did not tell them that I was pregnant. I draped my sari in a way to completely disguise my slowly swelling stomach. No one noticed anything unusual, except that, one day, my new Mistress laughingly observed, "Roshni, you waddle like a duck. I think all the rice you eat goes to your stomach and settles there. You are getting quite a little paunch, you know." I was too frightened to answer, but from then on I took extra care to cover myself well to camouflage the baby growing inside me.

I continued cleaning pots and pans, washing clothes and wiping floors on my hands and knees. I often ended up with backache and swollen feet, but of course, I did not dare complain as I needed the job. I usually got up early, gave my Master and Mistress tea and biscuits in bed, and then started sweeping the floor. But that morning I awoke while it was still dark and felt water trickling down my legs.

My first thought was that I had somehow wet myself while asleep. But soon the pains started, slow at first, but becoming more intense and frequent, until it felt as if the bones in my lower back would shatter. I lay on a mat on the floor and felt a warm gush of blood flow out between my legs. The pain was excruciating. My thighs were quivering uncontrollably. I bit down hard on my lips to stop myself from screaming out loud, and felt the salty taste of blood on my tongue. Suddenly, the pain receded and I felt that everything inside me wanted to get out. I felt this great urge to push. So I took a deep breath and pushed and pushed and pushed. Then all was darkness.

I must have lost consciousness, for when I woke the pain was gone and I was lying in a pool of blood. The baby, covered in blood and *fuzz*, was squirming at my feet. I have seen many babies being born in the slums and so I knew what had to be done. I took an old razor blade discarded by my Master, and cut the long, slimy cord running from the baby's navel to the dark purple flaccid lump floating in the pool of blood. My grandmother had once told me that it is called the "flower", and even then I had asked why such an ugly thing should be given such a lovely name. Grandmother had said, "Because it is the miracle of life, child."

I did not quite agree with Grandmother. I finally took a match and seared the end of the little piece of the cord I had left dangling at the baby's navel. Then I did what had to be done.

By now the sky was light and I heard my Mistress calling for me in an annoyed tone. I am never late serving their morning tea and I could hear her loudly wondering if I had fallen ill. She started knocking on my door, calling me incessantly by my name. I could not ignore her any longer. I dragged myself to my feet. I felt very weak and reeled drunkenly to the door. As I was covered with blood and the floor was a sea of red, I opened the door only a crack. She took one look at my white face and pushed the door open.

"What on earth is the matter with you Roshni?" asked my Mistress. "Are you alright? Are you unwell?"

I did not have answers to her questions. So I just moved aside so that she could look into the room. My perfectly formed, beautiful baby girl was floating in the sea of blood which I found hard to believe had all come from my body. Her dark, velvet-brown eyes stared upwards but saw nothing. Her little mouth, open for her first suckle, was frozen in a little "o".

She was dead. I had squeezed her soft little neck until she had choked, unable even to utter the first cry which announces the arrival of a newborn. I had killed her. For what need did the world have for another Roshni?

ASYLUM

"Go away, go away. Don't touch me. Who are these people? Why have they come to my room? Take them away, ayah. You know I don't like strangers."

The nurse in her coarse white sari with a thin black border running along the edge looked helplessly from the whimpering woman huddled in the corner of the room to the man accompanied by a nine-year old girl.

The girl was Ayesha and the man her father, whom her grandmother affectionately called Bablu. A creamy complexion and unusual hazel eyes made it clear even at nine that Ayesha would grow up to be a rare beauty. Her eyes probed inquisitively into everything around her. This was the first time Ayesha was visiting her mother, Suraiya, at the mental asylum where she had been committed seven years ago.

Ayesha had always known that her mother was a mental patient. Almost everyday her grandmother would tell Ayesha the story, repeating that it was all her mother's fault. When pregnant with Ayesha, her mother would take a shower every evening and, letting her long, dark tresses stream over her shoulders, would awkwardly make her way up the rather steep staircase to the roof of the house. The house was an old one dating from the British colonial period, and the flat spacious roof had thick walls like ramparts running along its four sides. Suraiya would walk on the roof for hours with the breeze blowing through her hair. She looked very beautiful and alluring, what with the special inner glow that pregnancy brought to some lucky women, and the wind silhouetting her body against the fine muslin saris that she so liked to wear. Ayesha's mother was one of those women whose swollen body and ripening breasts somehow made her look sensual, which was all the more attractive because she was totally unconscious of the effect.

"Time and again I warned your mother," her grandmother told Ayesha, as she sat braiding her granddaughter's hair. "Time and again I told her that it was a dangerous thing to walk in deepening twilight on rooftops, especially if you have long hair, and worse if you wear it loose and flowing. Everyone knows that it is at twilight that djinns hover between earth and heaven, ever on the lookout for possessing beautiful young women. But who pays attention to an old woman?" and, expressing her disapproval and indignation, her grandmother had tied an extra hard knot on the narrow black, cotton ribbon she used to secure the ends of Ayesha's plaits.

"Instead," continued Ayesha's grandmother, "Suraiya would laugh and tell me, '*Amma*, these are old wives' tales. Djinns have better things to do than come after me. I am into my ninth month and I feel so hot. The walk on the cool roof after the day's work really helps me. It is beautiful to see the trees turn black against the reddening sky and watch the crows flapping home to their nests. You should hear the sparrows, *Amma*, they create such a racket before turning in to sleep! And then all around little pinpoints of lights tell us another day has come to an end.' She would pause as if seeing everything in her mind's eye, and continue, 'Besides, the doctor did tell me that walking is very good during pregnancy, and where else can I walk if not on the roof? And when can I walk if not in the evening? During the day there's so much to be done around the house.'

"So what could I do?" her grandmother said, her lips red from chewing *paan*. "Modern women like your mother think they know everything. And look what happened. The very thing I feared happened. On one of her evening strolls, a djinn must have taken possession of her, for from the day you were born, she would not even look at you, leave alone give you the breast."

"*Hai, Hai*! What a disaster that was," and her grandmother smacked her forehead at the mere memory of that day. "A newborn baby and no milk to be found. We tried to pump out the milk from your mother's breasts, for it was easy to see they could feed ten babies, not one. But your mother would not let anyone touch her although milk was oozing out and soaking her blouse, the sheets, everything. And there you were screaming at the top of your lusty little lungs. Naturally, poor little baby, you were hungry and you wanted food," and her grandmother pinched her cheeks affectionately.

"At the end," Grandmother continued, "after sending people here and there, and everywhere, we found that our neighbour's maidservant had just had a baby. So we hired her as a wet nurse for you until you were old enough to drink out of a bottle. *Ma-go-ma!* What chaos and pandemonium it was at the time."

Her grandmother paused, lost in thought for a while. Then, sighing deeply, continued with her story, "Your mother would lie in bed for days just staring outside the window. Maybe she was looking at her trees and crows. Who knows? Doctors came and doctors went, but no one could say what was wrong with her. Of course they couldn't," ejaculated her grandmother, the gray knot on top of her head bristling with indignation. "Of course doctors could not find out what was wrong with her. She did not need a medical doctor. She needed a special *mulla* who had the power to exorcise djinns. I know for sure that she is under the influence of a djinn. But who listens to whom? Who pays any attention to an old woman? Not your father. Not those doctors.

"At the end what happened? Things got worse. There came a time when your mother wouldn't let anyone into the room, let alone near her. The situation became intolerable. Finally my poor, patient Bablu, your father, had no choice left but to send her to the *pagla garod*. They say no one is ever cured in these lunatic asylums," mused her grandmother, speaking more to herself than to Ayesha. Then, coming out of her reverie, she added, "But what is God's will is God's will. Run along now and play and don't get yourself too dirty."

Standing in the asylum, Ayesha did not experience any special emotions as she looked at her mother cowering in the corner with her face buried in her arms. Suraiya was dressed in a printed cotton sari. Her hair, still long and lustrous, was disheveled. But she was clean and smelt faintly of the cheap, strongly perfumed talcum powder very popular in the market at the time. Her room was bare but for a thick mattress on the floor which, although old and cracked in places, was shiny from years of scrubbing and swabbing. Sunlight flooded through a high, barred window which was free of dust and cobwebs. To Ayesha her mother was nothing but a stranger who had not heeded her wise old grandmother's repeated warnings and, because of her stubbornness, now the whole family was suffering. Annoyance and resentment welled up inside her. She could not understand why her father still felt so deeply for this woman who did not even recognize him.

No, that was not quite true. Ayesha had some idea of her father's love for her mother, for her grandmother had told Ayesha in great detail the romantic way that her father had met her mother. Bablu had fallen desperately in love with Suraiya the very first time he had seen her in the market buying yellow and green glass bangles to match the sari she was wearing at the time. A sheet of hair fell over her face as she examined each bangle to make sure that it was not cracked, but well-welded to form a complete circle. When satisfied, she had slipped on one bangle at a time, squeezing her soft hands to ease the bangle over. Her sparkling eyes and the smile escaping from her lips showed her pleasure at the task. She first put on a yellow bangle, then a green, then a yellow, then a green until her whole arm was encircled with bright spirals of coloured glass. Supremely pleased with herself, she had laughed delightedly and, jingling and jangling, had hailed the nearest rickshaw.

Ayesha's father had unashamedly pursued the rickshaw on his bicycle, anxious not to lose her, and determined to find out who she was and where she lived. After that it was only a matter of time. Bablu had good prospects. He was a teacher in a local college. Suraiya's parents were dead and her brother, who was her guardian, was only too happy and relieved to have received such a marriage proposal for his sister.

Of course, Ayesha's grandmother had always had her misgivings. "Just look at your father's antics," she said one day to Ayesha while carving slices of ginger to add to the mango chutney she was making. "He sees a strange girl in the market, follows her home and then comes and tells me that he will marry her and no one else. At that time he did not even know her name. Mad boy."

So thin that they were nearly transparent, daisy-shaped slices of ginger spilled out of her grandmother's clever knife. "I had warned your father even then that beautiful girls are well and good, but mark my words, they always create a lot of headache."

Running her hands through the little pile of ginger daisies, and satisfied with her handiwork, Ayesha's grandmother had gathered the ginger in her fist and tossed them into the pot of bubbling syrup. "But who listens to whom? Your father always was headstrong. And look what happened. No one can blame me for not warning Bablu of the consequences. But God's will is God's will and what will happen will happen."

Today's visit to the asylum was, however, a special one. Ayesha's grandmother had died a year ago and everyone advised her father that it was unwise of Bablu to try and bring up a daughter in a woman-less house. One could not trust ayahs and maidservants nowadays, and Bablu's relatives had their own families to take care of and couldn't spare time for Ayesha. Realizing that his friends spoke the truth, Bablu had reluctantly agreed to marry a second time. Besides, he really missed the love and care he had received first from Suraiya and then from his mother. But before taking the final step, he had come to see if by some miracle Suraiya had become her old self again.

Her mother's screams at the sight of her father and herself had dashed whatever little hope Bablu had harboured. Absentmindedly stroking Ayesha's hair, her father had stared disconsolately at the woman on the floor, trying to find the happy, carefree girl with the yellow and green glass bangles. He knew she was there somewhere inside of this stranger, but who had the key to let her out? He shook the tears from his eyes and, taking Ayesha by the hand said, "Come Ma, there is nothing we can do here except pray for the peace of her mind."

He gave Suraiya's ayah a generous tip and repeated several times to take good care of her. The ayah, who had been in charge of Ayesha's mother from the very first day that she had been brought to the asylum, sadly shook her head and said, "What a beauty she was when she had first come to us. Now look at her."

Visitors to the asylum were few and far between and the ayah wanted to make full use of this opportunity. She hurriedly continued, "*Sahib*, you are one of the very few people who come to visit their relatives in the asylum. Most people deposit the poor crazed person with us and never come back. They prefer to think that that the person no longer exists. Sometimes they do not even come to claim the dead body. When that happens we send the corpse to the local teaching hospital. They always need bodies for students to dissect."

Suddenly realizing that Ayesha's father was anxious to leave, the ayah quickly added, " Don't mind my saying this Sahib, but you have been very faithful to poor Suraiya for many, many years. You are young and can give many brothers and sisters to our Ayesha here. You should remarry and start your life all over again. At the end we are all in Allah's hands."

Soon after, through the good graces of his friends, Nahar was introduced to Bablu as a prospective wife. Nahar was a widow whose husband had died recently. She had no children because her husband had been impotent. But to hide his shame, her husband had put all the blame on Nahar, telling friends and family that she was barren and incapable of bearing children. It was only because he was kindhearted and felt sorry for Nahar that he did not throw her out of the house and marry a second time. Nahar came from a poor family and had never been to school. So she allowed her husband to perpetuate the falsehood which kept his macho image alive in front of friends and family.

Nahar's acquiescence to this arrangement however seemed to have increased her husband's frustrations. As the years went by, he took to drinking heavily, and giving Nahar a sound thrashing with or without any provocation on her part. He could be aroused to anger by such innocuous things as Nahar being less than prompt at bringing him his slippers. Or it could be that the curry was not heated to his specifications. So one night, when two policemen came and told Nahar that her husband had been killed in a road accident, her first reaction was to send up a silent prayer of gratitude to God for releasing her from this bondage.

However, bad as her marital experience had been, Nahar knew that she could not continue long in her state of independent widowhood. Her husband's small savings would not really last too long, and not having any children to give her some status, she would be viewed with suspicion and disapproval by society as a whole. So when she was told about Ayesha's father, the existence of a first wife in a lunatic asylum did not particularly worry her. Her immediate thought was that at least Bablu was neither impotent nor sterile. If she could have even one child by him, she would have a purpose in life, no matter what kind of a person Bablu turned out to be.

But Nahar was lucky. Bablu turned out to be kind and gentle and very soon Nahar gave birth to twin daughters. As the girls grew up it became obvious to Nahar that they would be as plain as herself. Where at first she had thought being a mother was self-fulfillment in itself, she now began to harbour resentment that if Allah in his goodness saw it fit to give her daughters, then He should have also made sure that they were at least pretty, if not beautiful. She began to begrudge Ayesha her golden skin and melting eyes. Nahar felt deeply embittered when friends and relatives openly fussed over Ayesha's beauty, hardly sparing a glance for the twins.

Maternal instincts are strange things. They can change a perfectly ordinary woman into a vicious animal if she feels that her offspring are being threatened. If the woman is by nature an extrovert, she will most likely attack her victim in the open like a tiger. If she is schemish by nature, she will behave more like the poisonous cobra, striking without warning from deep, hidden recesses. Nahar was a cobra. Her resentment against Ayesha grew daily but she took great care to hide her feelings from the young girl.

By the time Ayesha was fourteen years old, her stepmother's hate and jealousy had become an obsession. Nahar felt that Bablu and his mother had spoilt Ayesha. The girl was arrogant and did not even try to please her stepmother. And Nahar was not far from the truth. Always doted on by her grandmother and her father, Ayesha had grown up feeling very special. Her father had told her, and he had never lied to her before, that he was marrying Nahar only so that there would be someone to take care of Ayesha and her father. So Ayesha felt that it was really Nahar's job to make sure that she and her father were happy.

Poor Ayesha. She was too young to understand how the game of life is played. How politics of relationships between husband and wife can bring about a shift in power and control, a control which could be overt or could be from behind the scenes. Ayesha was unaware of the depth of the resentment and hatred that Nahar harboured against her. She was unaware of the net that Nahar was weaving around her, a net that would deprive her of her freedom, crush her arrogance, and make her realize that she was special only if the person in control of the household thought her to be so.

Nahar's strategy was simple. Ayesha must be married off as soon as possible. Bablu would not readily welcome the idea and so it was essential for Nahar to choose the right moment for broaching the subject. Luck was on her side, and Nahar soon got the opportunity she was looking for.

Bablu had just returned from a week spent in the village for his research work. The roads had been treacherous, and the day hot and steamy. He was exhausted. He now lay stretched out in bed dressed in a thin cotton *kurta* and a gray-and-black checked *lungi* loosened at the waist. Nahar settled herself at the foot of the bed and nestled both his feet in her sari-draped lap. Gently but firmly she started kneading his heels with her hands.

Ayesha's father gave a sigh of contentment and stretched himself like a cat, "You spoil me thoroughly, Nahar," he said.

"Beloved," Nahar cooed softly, "You just do not know how good and noble you are. You have restored my faith in men. If my previous husband were still alive, I am sure I would not have been able to survive his vicious beatings, and would have been dead and buried in a white *kafan* a long time ago. I have plenty to be grateful to you for, and nothing I do can be enough to show my gratitude."

Bablu closed his eyes, sensuously digging his feet deeper into his wife's lap. Nahar leaned back, pushed up her pelvis and started to gently grind her hips. She saw that she had succeeded in arousing her husband.

"You know, dear," she said, being careful not to break her rhythm. "Ayesha is growing up fast and looks much older than her fourteen years. Times are bad. More and more one hears about rape cases, or about some hooligan throwing acid on a young girl's face simply because she had spurned his advances. I remain tense and worried about Ayesha all the time. Perhaps it might not be a bad idea to look for a good bridegroom for her."

Mildly annoyed at having to think about anything else but the warm, deep promises of his wife's lap, Bablu protested equably, "Ayesha is too young. She must first complete her studies."

"Of course she must complete her studies. I would be the first to say that a woman must be educated so that she is able to stand on her own two feet. Don't I know from my own miserable experience the importance of a girl's education? I want as much as you, or perhaps even more than you, that Ayesha should graduate. But we must also be practical. Ayesha can easily continue her studies after marriage. Nowadays many mothers-in-law encourage their sons' wives to continue their education. You see, once she is married, there is little chance of her being harassed by the street Romeo's, and anyway the responsibility of her protection would then be her husband's not ours."

A few more of such strategically timed arguments, and Nahar was able to convince Bablu about getting Ayesha married soon.

The rest was simple. Finding a bridegroom for such a beautiful girl was no problem at all. They finally settled on Anwar who, his family said, had recently returned to the country after completing his studies abroad. His father had a small, but well-established, business. Everyone thought that Ayesha was extremely lucky to have made such a match.

Independent-minded Ayesha, however, did not at all agree. She swore that she would starve to death rather than get married now. Her grandmother had foreseen that Ayesha would get many academic degrees and become one of the most famous women in the country. How could Ayesha do all that if she had to cook, have babies and take care of her husband and in-laws?

Affectionate as ever, her father gently convinced her, "*Ma*, times are bad. I am only a college teacher. I cannot afford to hire a servant who will accompany you to school and back. And anyway, even servants cannot be trusted nowadays. Your stepmother and I worry about you day and night. I know you are very young, but I assure you that you will be allowed to complete you education after you are married. I have made this a part of the marriage contract. So don't worry, *Ma*, you will graduate one day. God willing, you will make a name for yourself, and one day when I open the newspapers," and Bablu smiled trying to calm down his beautiful, clever, agitated daughter, "I will see your face under a heading in large letters saying that Mrs. Ayesha So-and-So has achieved brilliant results and broken such-and-such record!"

Too late, Ayesha saw the trap that her stepmother had prepared for her. Bablu may have the final say in all matters, but Ayesha recognized her stepmother's behind-the-scenes manipulations which convinced her father into making this decision about her marriage. Impotent to escape the trap, Ayesha burst into angry tears and fled to her room screaming, "If *Dadima* were alive she would never have allowed this to happen."

Visibly shaken at the reminder of his dead mother, Bablu turned to follow Ayesha. But Nahar put out a hand and gently drew him to a chair. "Sit down, Ayesha's father," she said, "There is no need to go running after her. Girls often react like this when they first hear about marriage. Young, headstrong girls like Ayesha will, of course, throw tantrums when they feel that their wishes are being thwarted. Give her time, and she will calm down and accept your decision. Once she is married and finds the pleasures of married life with Anwar, she will settle down and be happy. It is every woman's *karma* to be married, have a family, and take care of her husband. I bless her with my *duas* that Anwar makes her as happy as you have made me."

"How wise you are, Nahar," said Bablu, easing himself into the chair, relieved to have the problem of a hysterical Ayesha taken off his hands. "It never fails to amaze me that, in spite of your terrible experience with your first husband, you are not bitter about life. The concern you have for Ayesha, your stepdaughter, is really praiseworthy."

Ayesha alternately sulked and cried on her wedding day, but it is hard to mar the perfection of a lotus coming to full bloom. She looked radiant and Nahar felt secretly reassured that she had done the right thing by pushing Ayesha out of the house. Now people could not compare her plain little girls to this beauty. Now her little girls, the centre of her existence, would not fall under the umbra of luminescent Ayesha. With Ayesha around they would surely have grown up to be psychological cases. Yes, Nahar had definitely done the right thing in getting Ayesha married and out of her house.

But for all man's plans and schemes, only that transpires which has been willed by God, Allah, Providence, or Fate, call a rose by any name.

One night, a few months after Ayesha's wedding, good, kind, gentle Bablu went to sleep and never woke up. Nahar had risen as usual and, after placing a cup of tea on Bablu's bedside table, had gone off to prepare breakfast. From the kitchen she heard the bedroom alarm clock go off at six o'clock because Bablu had to be in college by eight. She heard the alarm peter off into tinny silence as the little key completely unwound itself. She shook her head, Bablu had again forgotten to turn off the alarm before going in for his shower. Nahar continued to crisply fry the *parathas*. She would later make some omlettes. This was Bablu's favourite breakfast.

When she had laid the food on the table, and Bablu had still not come out briskly rubbing his hair with a towel as he usually did, Nahar walked impatiently into the bedroom admonishing Bablu that he would be late for college. She found him with his eyes closed and smiling, perhaps at a young girl trying on green and yellow glass bangles. A little house lizard had dropped from the ceiling and was curiously exploring his face.

And what of our Ayesha?

Feeling desperately alone and abandoned after her father died, Ayesha one morning broached to her husband, the subject of her returning to school. "You know," she said, as Anwar got ready to go to work, "I have already missed a lot of my classes and should be going back to school soon."

"I'll talk to my father about it," mumbled Anwar fixing his tie and not meeting Ayesha's eyes.

That evening her father-in-law called Ayesha to him. He was reclining in an easy chair and a little servant boy was massaging his feet. The boy was the gardener's son and worked in the house in exchange for food and lodging.

"A woman's place is in her home," he admonished her, first gently and then more harshly, as he saw Ayesha's face set in stubborn lines. "Anwar needs you in the house. Your getting a *BA* or an *MA* degree is of no interest or consequence to us. My status and my son's status in society are of our own making. Your degrees will not add anything to it. You can read and write, and that is enough.

"Besides," he added, "You are much too beautiful. Young boys will be chasing you everywhere, and who knows what you may be tempted to do? No, it is best that you stay at home and take care of Anwar, your mother-in-law and myself."

And closing his eyes, he started pulling on his hookah. The subject was closed and there was nothing more to be discussed.

Confined to the role of a caregiver, Ayesha felt the noose around her neck tighten another notch. But deep in misery as she was, Ayesha began to notice a change coming over her husband. Anwar began to have sudden swings in mood. From being hyperactive, when he would turn on the music full blast and dance late into the night, he would slump into deep depression, lying morose and comatose for days. At times, Anwar seemed not to recognize Ayesha. At times without any provocation Anwar would pick up books and throw them at Ayesha, and even try to throttle her.

One day, managing to escape from Anwar's clutches and thoroughly frightened, she ran to her father-in-law. "*Abba, Abba,*" she choked and shuddered, "There is something seriously wrong with Anwar. You must show him to a doctor."

Anwar's father placidly pulled on his hookah and said, "There is nothing to be concerned about, Daughter-in-law. It is an old problem and it is called schizophrenia. The doctors recommended that Anwar would get better if he got married. Give him time and he will recover fully. I told you he needs you at home. You must take good care of him and make sure he takes all his medications on time. Your mother-in-law is getting on in years. She cannot look after Anwar as she used to."

Waiting until Anwar had fallen into an exhausted sleep, Ayesha crept into her bedroom. She pulled down the heavy, gold-lettered dictionary her father had presented her for standing first in her class. She looked up the word schizophrenia. She did not know the spelling and looked up every word under the letter "s" until she found it. Pulling the table lamp a little closer, she read in a shocked whisper, the words choking in her throat, "Dementia praecox or kindred form of insanity marked by introversion and loss of connection between thoughts and actions." Then she looked up introversion. She closed the dictionary and carefully put it back in the bookshelf.

She glanced out the window and saw the mad woman who lived under the banyan tree by the roadside. She was picking lice from her hair and talking to herself. She was usually naked, but today someone had taken pity on her, and had thrown a hessian sack over her for modesty. Her emaciated arms and legs stuck out like leathery sticks, the soles of her feet cracked and engrained with grime.

Ayesha looked from her husband lying prone on the bed, to the mad beggar under the tree. She made up her mind. From her wardrobe she pulled out a yellow and green cotton sari and let down her long hair just like her mother used to do so many years ago. She couldn't find any matching glass bangles and did not want to waste too much time looking.

Dressed to her liking, she quietly slipped out of the house and hailed a passing rickshaw, "Take me to the *pagla garod*, please." The rickshawalah looked at her charily, but she seemed normal enough. So he hitched up his *lungi*, swung himself into the seat, and pedaled towards the old part of town.

At the *pagla garod*, Ayesha waited until the rickshawallah was out of sight. Then she ripped her sari and blouse and ran her hands through her hair so that they fell in strands over her face. Satisfied that she looked sufficiently like the deranged beggar she had seen from her bedroom window, Ayesha beat loudly and repeatedly on the door of the mental asylum.

The door was opened by her mother's ayah who stared at the vision mouth agape.

"I am Ayesha," giggled Ayesha, pretending to pick lice from her hair and shoo imaginary flies from her face. "I have come to join my mother. They say like mother, like daughter." And she burst into peals of laughter.

Finally recognizing her for the girl she had seen some five years ago, the ayah put an arm around Ayesha's shoulder and drew her into the room. "Ssh, Ssh, Ma. It's alright, you will be safe here." said the ayah, as she bolted and latched the heavy wooden door shutting out the world.

Ayesha's father-in-law sat in his easy chair pulling on his hookah. He was surrounded by friends and relatives. "Very sad, very sad," said an aged uncle, "Who knew that Ayesha would have to be sent off to a lunatic asylum? What a scandal!"

"What else can you expect?" asked Ayesha's father-in-law. "Her mother has been a mental patient for years. It is not at all surprising that Ayesha has followed her mother's footsteps. They say it is hereditary, you know."

The hookah bubbled as he pulled on it long and deep.

THE PARTY

The hand-cut crystal chandelier glittered down upon the select group of people sitting on the pastel-hued Isphahan carpet woven in an intricate pattern of floral vines. It sparked off the diamonds and heavy gold jewelry worn by the women and glowed on the gold and silver of their rich silk saris. It flashed on the brass buttons of army uniforms, and on the spiky spurs of boots worn by the men.

The women sat relaxed and graceful on the floor. Some sat with legs pulled up under their chins and feet decorously covered by swathes of expensive silk. Others sat with backs against walls or conveniently placed sofas, their legs neatly tucked in sideways and out of sight.

It was the men who were uncomfortable in their western suits and full-dress uniforms. Their stiff jackets, narrow trousers and spurred boots did not allow them to find a comfortable position. At times they stretched out their legs to get some relief but pulled them up again soon: it was considered quite rude to be pointing your feet at anyone, and, in the crowded room, it was impossible to avoid doing so. They shifted this way and that to ease their cramped muscles but they had little choice. It was the President's wish to sit on the floor and listen to songs rendered by those present. And those present were the embassy officers, their wives, and the entourage which accompanied the President on this grand state visit.

The stiffly formal reception by the host country, which was attended by anyone who was anyone, was over, and the President, feeling he had admirably withstood his share of the day's suffering for his people and his country, wanted to relax and enjoy the rest of the evening. The President was a four-star general who had taken over the country during a military coup. Since then he had regularized his position and established a kind of democracy in order to placate aid-giving western countries who strongly opposed military governments. The democracy was superficial only, and the President held full power to do almost anything he wished.

The Ambassador was a shrewd and experienced government servant who had done his homework on the President and was fully conversant with his likes and dislikes. Also, the Ambassador shared the President's sentiments that after such formal receptions one really needed some distraction. So the embassy staff and the members of the President's entourage congregated at the Ambassador's house where everything stood in readiness for the President's pleasure.

Smartly dressed waiters in white livery with gold buttons and braids bent over double to serve drinks and salted nuts to those seated on the floor. For the President there was the very special and very expensive 25-year-old Black Dog whiskey, for he was very discriminating about his scotch and would drink nothing else. A bottle of the rich gold liquid, together with a Waterford crystal tumbler, stood on a highly polished Christofel silver tray on the floor next to the President. No water, soda or ice was needed. The President was in complete agreement with connoisseurs of scotch. The only way to take such mature and smooth whiskey was at room temperature, neat and unadulterated. A minor general of the army kept replenishing the President's glass.

The Ambassador's wife also liked her scotch neat but she was not so discriminating. Short of rice toddy, she was game for anything. Today she had indulged a little too much because the tension of the Presidential visit could only be endured under an alcohol-induced haze. For weeks before the visit her husband, a vicious rude man at the best of times, had been impossible to talk to and intolerable to live with. He snapped and foul-mouthed everyone from the Minster

Counselor to the gardener. In a way one could not quite blame him altogether for, if anything, anything at all, displeased the President during the visit, the Ambassador was sure to lose his job. Even so, in spite of the more than twenty years of a shared life, the Ambassador's wife could not withstand her husband's boorish behaviour without an alcoholic buffer.

The thought of leaving him had occasionally crossed her mind. But where would she go? What choices did she have in her life? She had only minimal education and no money of her own. Her parents were dead and if she walked out on her husband, her brothers would certainly not welcome her in their not so well-to-do households. The question of seeking refuge with her sister, who was quite well off, of course did not arise. It was not done. She could lay some claim on her brothers though, because hadn't she relinquished to them all claims to her share of the little house her father had built in the village?

She herself, while once very beautiful — which was why the Ambassador had chosen to marry her in spite of her poor parentage — was rather jaded now. The regular bouts of heavy drinking, while helping to dull the pain of seeing her beauty disappear day by day, did little to preserve the very thing that she saw slipping away from her. So who, in his right mind, would want to marry her now?

Besides, she doted on her children and had she left him, her husband would have been sure to keep them from meeting her. And he would be backed both by law and society. And anyway, life could be worse. She enjoyed the many parties they attended, delighted in the beautiful clothes and jewelry which her husband bought for her because he thought she had to be suitably dressed as the wife of such a senior ranking officer as himself. And, if at times she found her husband's behaviour intolerable, a bottle from the shiny, well-stocked bar always helped bring things back in perspective. It also helped her to overcome her inhibitions about some of the things she was forced to do to advance her husband's career.

However, nothing she ate or drank could dull the stab of pain she felt when she saw the new Third Secretary and his young wife walk into the room. He was on his first foreign posting, and she knew that he had joined the Foreign Service with full faith in a system that did not exist, innocently unaware that, like it or not, he and his wife were part of deadly games where winner takes all. She knew only too well that the Ambassador was very skillful at playing these games, for she had seen the outcome in several of their postings, both at home and abroad. She also knew that she herself had little influence over her husband, and even less power to change the causes and consequences.

"Oh, what's the use," thought the Ambassador's wife, shrugging mentally, "What will be will be," and giggling, sidled up a little closer to the President.

He ran his hands over her silk-covered thighs and asked, "Who is that beautiful young thing in purple?"

"Oh, that is just the new Third Secretary's wife," replied the Ambassador's wife, pretending nonchalance. "They have just joined the embassy and have been married only two months. Very inexperienced," she added discouragingly.

The Ambassador sitting cross-legged on the other side of the President overheard the exchange and volunteered, "But Mr. President, Sir, she sings like the *koel*, a nightingale she is, no less. If you wish, I will send her to the State Guest House tonight, to sing specially for you."

In spite of her alcoholic daze, the Ambassador's wife tried desperately to intervene. "But darling," she addressed her husband in the western fashion that he found so smart. "Darling, it is Zulfia who is the accomplished singer and who should be given the honour and privilege of singing specially for the President."

Emptying his glass and squeezing the Ambassador's wife's knees, the President asked, "And who on earth is Zulfia?"

The Ambassador's wife pointed to a slim woman who was laughingly protesting, but only verbally, about someone's arms round her waist. The end of her black chiffon sari had slipped off her shoulder and had fluttered to the floor. She made no attempt to pull it back up to cover her décolletage exposed in a provocatively designed blouse.

"Her husband is the Economic Counselor. See, there he is, asleep in the corner. He has no head for drinks," giggled the Ambassador's wife, pointing to a bald man with a generous paunch who was sitting slumped against the far wall, snoring gently.

"Well, she is nowhere near the Third Secretary's wife in looks, but seems willing to play ball," observed the President shrewdly.

"Sir, Mr. President," interposed the Ambassador, immediately sensing the President's interest in Zulfia, "I shall personally order Zulfia to sing for you tonight. But tomorrow night our little *koel* in purple will pay you a surprise visit."

Once more out-manoeuvered by her husband and feeling sick to her stomach, the Ambassador's wife turned blindly to the Colonel sitting by her side. Pressing herself against him, she said, "Why don't you get me a fresh drink, hm?"

Sitting cross-legged on the carpet in front of the President, Zulfia pulled the box-like harmonium to her. She ran her right hand up and down the keys, and with her left hand pumped the accordion-like bellows of the instrument. She began to sing in a clear voice, popular classical songs and ballads whose lyrics sent the men into paroxysms of frenzy, arousing them to repeatedly call for encores. The cries of "*Wah, wah*" and "*Shahbash*" wafted out into the garden twinkling with garlands of miniature lights which had been put up for the occasion.

To provide Zulfia with some respite one or two of the men sang songs of Rabindranath Tagore, but they sounded dull and dragging after Zulfia's enthusiastic rendition of *gazals*. Even well-known film songs when sung by others sounded muted. The Third Secretary's wife was also pulled into the centre of the circle. With her husband beaming proudly at her, she sang in an appealing, but untrained voice, a ballad written by the great Bengali poet Nazrul Islam. But over and over again, the harmonium was pushed to Zulfia, and over and over again, she rose to the occasion and belted out songs until the very rafters rang with thunderous applause.

At last the President stretched out his legs and announced that he wished to retire for the night. In a flurry of movement, soft rustlings of silk, and harsh jangling of spurs, everyone got off the floor with as much semblance of sobriety as individual conditions allowed. The President stood up swaying on his feet, and was quickly supported by his Aide-de-Camp on one side and by his favourite General on the other. All three entered the gleaming Mercedes Benz limousine which, with flags flying rigidly on either side, swished out of the driveway. The Mercedes was accompanied by outriders on motorbikes, a whining police car leading the convoy and another bringing up the rear. The Ambassador and his wife followed in another Mercedes, while the entourage scrambled to find their transports, everyone in a rush to reach the State Guest House, if possible, before the President arrived, so that they could be there to receive him. Zulfia and her harmonium followed in the embassy staff car. Oblivious to the world, her husband slept on in the corner of the now empty sitting room.

Next morning the Ambassador called the new Third Secretary to his office and told him that the President had especially praised his wife's singing, and had mentioned that he would like to hear her sing some more. She should therefore be ready to go to the State Guest House tonight, immediately after the bilateral dinner which was being held at the Ambassadorial Residence.

Flattered and pleased at the attention the Third Secretary said, "Sir, I will immediately arrange for the staff car to take us to the State Guest House tonight."

The Ambassador looked at him coldly and in an exasperated voice said, "Don't be a fool. She will go alone."

That evening the long dining table which seated twenty four was covered with a stiffly-starched, white damask tablecloth. Earlier that morning the butler had ironed the massive tablecloth and stored it in a roll to prevent unseemly creases. The heavy, intricately carved silver gleamed from the extra special polish it had received for the occasion, and the Bohemian hand-cut crystal gave out rainbow sparks whenever the pendulous chandelier trembled in the breeze.

The formal china with the official crest and seal sat imposingly on the table, while an extravaganza of roses, chrysanthemums and lilies added colour to the white, silver and crystal display. Tall, antique, silver and crystal candelabra complemented the chandelier and cast a warm glow over the august gathering.

Only one place way down at the bottom of the table was empty. It was a little awkward for those sitting on either side of the empty chair because when his only neighbour was talking to his neighbour he had no one to talk to and had to sit looking intelligent and pretend not to be bored. The Ambassador noted the empty seat and looked round the table for the Third Secretary. He was sitting at his designated place with downcast eyes, staring down at his plate and not speaking to anyone.

The dinner commenced and one course followed another with easy grace. The Ambassador's wife was a past master at choosing menus and arranging parties to suit every occasion. The cook outdid himself and the waiters performed faultlessly. The Ambassador's wife did not have to lift her eyebrows even once to indicate her displeasure at some lapse in serving etiquette which she had been drumming into the staff for the last week or so. Toasts were drunk, and the President expressed his great pleasure at the success of his visit. He complimented the Ambassador on his superb diplomatic achievements and the Ambassador's wife for her excellence as the perfect hostess. Nothing marred the evening except the one empty seat.

The next day the President left for his own country, and the Ambassador heaved a sigh of relief for a visit successfully concluded. It was no mean achievement even if he did say so himself.

The following Diplomatic Bag brought three letters for the Ambassador. One informed him about a promotion for Zulfia's husband. The second was a transfer order of the Ambassador to an obscure post usually covered by a Charge d'Affaires. The third was a letter dismissing the Third Secretary from the service quoting an obscure military regulation which in special circumstances was applicable to civilians as well.

The President could not abide anyone who could not fulfill a promise, even if he was a successful diplomat and did his job well. In fact, it was only the overwhelming success of the visit that prevented the President from outright dismissing the Ambassador, even if he was personally inclined to do so. However, no such considerations stood in the way in the case of the Third Secretary. The President despised even more, those upstarts who either pretended not to understand the subtleties of games played in high circles, or had the gall to defy implicit orders of a Head of State.

THE PROSTITUTE

Mariam was a prostitute. She had never known any other kind of life. Her mother had been a prostitute when Mariam was a child, and when she turned fourteen Mariam had taken up the profession so that her mother could spend the rest of her days in prayer and meditation.

Mariam was also very beautiful. She had thick dark hair falling in waves to her waist, and it gave her great pleasure when her mother oiled and perfumed it daily before Mariam took her bath. Her skin was smooth, golden and unblemished and her eyes an unusual hazel. Maybe some ancestor had come from the northern part of the country or even perhaps had been a foreigner.

Mariam did not particularly mind having to sleep with so many different men to earn her livelihood. Ever since a child, she had seen all the young women around her do the same. Since she was beautiful and had a certain air of polish, she was always in demand and so managed to earn quite a handsome amount each month. She paid the room rent plus a commission regularly each month to the old man who owned the three-storey house and in return was allowed to occupy a room without much interference from him.

In fact, compared to some of the others, Mariam's room was stately and was spacious enough to partition off into two parts. True, the partition made of woven bamboo mat was rather flimsy, but at least her mother did not have to sleep outside in the verandah every time Mariam entertained a client. The room was in the corner of the third floor and overlooked some *krishnachura* trees. The view changed seasonally from a riot of flaming red, crinkly blossoms to the soft, whispery green of the feathery leaves. And when the stormy nor'westers blew heralding the monsoon rains, the trees stood out in stark contrast against the lowering grey sky. It gave her profound satisfaction and she felt a new zest for life every time she witnessed some particularly spectacular display of thunder and lightening. To Mariam watching the different moods of the elements outside her window was like watching God at play.

Life for Mariam was not too bad. She and her mother had two square meals a day, a roof over their heads and even some savings which they kept locked in a little green tin trunk with a pink rose painted on the lid. The key to the trunk was knotted to the end of her mother's *sari* and perpetually hung over her shoulder. The trunk contained all their precious belongings which included her mother's wedding *sari* and two gold bangles which her mother had had made for Mariam when she was only four years old.

By and large most of the men treated her kindly. If sometimes a drunken client was troublesome and Mariam had to suffer some beatings, she took these as the hazards of her job. Her mother collected the payments before a client entered her room, and the regulars frequently added a generous tip. These were the well-to-do gentlemen who obviously came from good homes and decent backgrounds. She sometimes wondered if they had any wives and if the wives were aware of their husbands' sojourns. Mariam neither envied these women for having husbands and homes, nor did she feel sorry that their husbands were cheating on them. In her experience the fact of life was that as long as men were men, women would get the short end of the stick one way or another.

She remembered the stormy night she and her mother had arrived in the city from their village. She could not have been more than five years old. Her father had married a second time and had driven her mother out because she could not bear him any more children. To her father it was imperative that he have a son to carry on his name, otherwise he could not look his younger brother in the face. Her uncle daily flaunted his two healthy sons in front of her father and was already eyeing the choice plot of land near the river because Mariam's grandfather was on his deathbed. Her uncle was readying himself to lay claim to the property arguing that he had a greater right to it as Mariam's father had no male issue.

Legally her uncle could not claim the whole property, but Mariam's father was not going to wait around to find out what the *shalish* would rule because he knew that the strong patriarchal culture prevalent in the village, reinforced by adequate financial incentives to the group of village elders, could secure a decision in favour of his brother. It was far better to ensure that he himself sired a male child. Now that she was older, Mariam could well understand the social pressures that prompted her father's actions. But that did not take away the pain of humiliation and abject poverty which resulted from the rejection and abandonment.

That terrible night Mariam and her mother had found their soaking wet way to a distant cousin of her mother's who had a hovel in a slum just on the outskirts of the town. Her mother's cousin, who herself lived hand to mouth, was too poor to support them, and so the next day she had introduced Mariam's mother to the old man who rented out rooms in that special part of the town. The cousin, however, omitted to explain to Mariam's mother what was expected of those who occupied these rooms because she knew that Mariam's mother was not as yet ready to work as a prostitute. But the cousin was practical and knew that when Mariam's mother realized that she had no other choice she would soon learn to accept the situation.

Fresh from the village and naively innocent, Mariam's mother could not at first fully grasp the implications of living in such an area. When men knocked on her door and made propositions to her, she indignantly slammed the door in their faces. Finally one day the old man, sitting as usual in his rattan easy chair and basking in the sun in his courtyard, called Mariam's mother to him. Very kindly and somewhat apologetically, he explained to her that if she did not pay the commission and the rent of the room by the end of the month, she and her daughter would be out in the street. Aware that she did not know anyone in the city and that she had no other way of earning money to pay the rent of the room and feed herself and her daughter, Mariam's mother was forced to accept the reality of her situation and succumbed to the will of Allah.

It had not been easy for her mother though. Mariam could recall nights when she would suddenly awake to find her mother sobbing quietly into the pillow just vacated by one more strange man. At that time, since they were new, the old man had given them the smallest room in the house, and Mariam had nowhere to go when her mother had to entertain a client. If it was still light outside, Mariam played in the street until her mother called her in. If it was dark she lay on a mat just outside her mother's door, most often asleep, but sometimes lying awake to hear the heavy breathings and the creaking of the old bed inside the room.

As Mariam grew older such things bothered her less and less. In fact, she actually looked forward to some of her mother's regular clients who sometimes brought her *batasha* in paper cones made out of old newsprint. The regulars knew that these tiny meringues made of sugar and egg white were a great favourite with Mariam. They had their eyes on her, for young as she was, she was already showing promises of becoming a great beauty.

Shaking herself out of her reverie, Mariam stretched pleasurably. Today was Friday, the Muslim sabbath, and the official weekly holiday. As a rule, no business was conducted on this day, and most of the men stayed home to look after family matters, do the household shopping, and attend the special congregation for the Friday prayers at the local mosques. So Mariam and the other girls reserved this day for giving a thorough cleaning to their rooms, for airing the bedclothes if it was not pouring with rain, for chatting with neighbours, and sometimes for even seeing a movie in the nearby movie theatre. Mariam seldom succeeded in persuading her mother to accompany her to the movies, but sometimes one of the girls living in the house would be quite willing to see the latest box-office hit.

It was quite a little ceremony going to the movies. Mariam and her friend would don their two-piece black silk *burkhas* which covered them from head to toe, shielding them from vulgar stares. The head dress, which was separate from the coat, fell over the shoulders and had a flap inset with a square of netting over the eyes so that they could look out without being looked at. The special occasion also called for hiring a rickshaw for taking them to the movie theatre where they would run up to the "Ladies" section especially reserved for women.

This section consisted of wooden benches running along a balcony which flanked one side of the screen so that to see the movie one had to sit sideways on the bench. The balcony was cordoned off by a black cloth screen which was lowered by a little boy just when the lights were dimmed and the show was about to start. The screen was quickly re-erected just before the lights went on again at interval time and at the end of the show. So the women were well protected from leers and lustful comments at all times.

Women enjoyed even more privileges. They did not have to queue up to buy tickets at the window. The little boy who attended to the cloth screen also had the duty to purchase tickets for the women who wanted to sit in the "Ladies." Mariam and her friend would send the boy to buy tickets as well as some sand-roasted peanuts from the vendor in front of the movie hall. Waiting for the movie to start, they would noisily crack open the warm nuts, expertly toss the kernals into their mouths, and drop the shells to join the litter on the floor deposited by some earlier movie goer. Then the movie would start and they would giggle and laugh at the comic parts, sigh during the romantic interludes and applaud loudly when the hero vanquished the villain and carried off the heroine in triumph.

It was also on Fridays that Mariam usually entertained her young visitors. They were the children of some of the women in the building and, because Mariam made a big fuss over them, they loved to visit her on her free day. She would oil and braid the little girls' hair and tell stories to the little boys, partly concocting from the movies she had seen and partly using her own imagination. She always kept a supply of her favourite *batasha* to give to the children when they came. She often wished that the children had something better to do than play all day long in the dusty street with the open, festering sewer running along the length of the road. But, as neither their mothers nor anyone else seemed bothered, Mariam saw little point in worrying about something over which she had little control.

It was just such a Friday, and Mariam was about to oil the hair of a little girl who was a particular favourite. She went to fetch the bottle where it stood warming in the sun so that the coconut oil, which congealed ever so quickly when stored in any cool place, would be runny enough to pour. As she stood bottle in hand, Mariam saw a group of ladies, some foreign, some local, get out of several cars and approach the house. Mouth agape, she could not begin to wonder what such women were doing in the neighbourhood, leave alone actually entering the brothel.

Full of curiosity she stood watching the women, the coconut oil in her hand beginning to turn cloudy as the bottle cooled. The local ladies had their heads decorously covered with the ends of their saris. The foreigners, instead of wearing dresses, had adopted the local garb and had on loose shirts and pajamas with long scarves fluttering round their necks. They seemed to be visiting rooms at random and talking to whomever they could find or whoever was willing to spare them any time.

Eventually the little group found their way to Mariam's room, and one of the ladies introduced herself, "I am Mrs. Hashem and with me are these ladies who are very concerned at the growing number of prostitutes in the city. We think it is a very degrading profession for women and also very damaging to society as a whole. We would like to take you away from this horrible environment and help you lead a decent life free from these humiliating and sinful surroundings. You are so young and beautiful. It is shameful that your mother not only condones such a profession but also lives off its income."

"But I have no other way of earning money," Mariam protested mildly, quite impressed by the fervour and dedication with which Mrs. Hashem spoke. "And if I don't work as a prostitute my mother and I will starve, you know."

"We are quite aware of that my child, and that is exactly why we are here," said Mrs. Hashem, beaming complacently at her own good intentions. Then, turning to the little girl who was still waiting patiently to have her hair oiled and braided by Mariam, she asked, "And who is this little girl? Is she your sister?"

"No, she is my neighbour's daughter," said Mariam.

"Does she live in the same room as her mother?" asked Mrs. Hashem. "What does she do when her mother has a man with her?"

"If she does not live with her mother where else would she live?" said Mariam, puzzled with the question and genuinely curious to know if there was any other solution to the problem. "When her mother is busy," Mariam continued, "like all the other children in the neighbourhood, she plays in the street or goes to sleep in the verandah outside her mother's room. If it rains, she naturally has to sleep inside the room because the verandah gets very wet."

Aghast and morally indignant at the state of affairs, and thoroughly convinced that they were doing the right thing in trying to stamp out prostitution, Mrs. Hashem turned to the other ladies and nodded emphatically, "Yes, we absolutely must do something immediately to change this intolerable situation."

The wind was sweeping the rain into the verandah, leaving it clean and glistening when Mrs. Hashem returned two weeks later. The damp edges of her sari clung to her ankles. The rain water, defying her umbrella trickled down her arms and dripped off her elbows.

Undaunted by such minor physical discomforts, and bolstered by her good intentions, she announced joyously and triumphantly, "I have been very busy. I have managed to find jobs for some of you in a garment factory which belongs to a friend of mine. You will be well paid, and places will be found for you to stay. You will be much better off than in this brothel of sin. You, Mariam, must come away with me.

I really cannot bear to see such innocent-looking beauty being soiled by this dreadful way of life. Be ready and I will come to fetch you and your mother early tomorrow morning."

The next day, uncertain about their decision, but unable to withstand Mrs. Hashem's moral onslaught, Mariam and her mother accompanied the lady to the garment factory where Mariam and another girl from the brothel were handed over to the owner of the factory. Having satisfactorily discharged her duty, Mrs. Hashem bustled away importantly to deliver the remaining girls to other places of work that she had found for them.

Mariam was led away to the work room of the factory where she observed everything in great astonishment. She saw the tired eyes of the women at the machines. She saw children cleaning up the debris littering the floor and running little errands down the sewing lines. The only familiar thing in this strange new alien world was the gleam in the men's eyes when they gazed at her.

The factory floor was a large hall with windows running down the length of one wall. Panes from several of the windows were missing and the gaping holes were stuffed with rags and remnants of brightly printed cloth which had been used to make shirts. Those windows which remained whole let in little light as they had become opaque with months of encrusted grime. Girls sat at electric sewing machines set in several rows in the centre of the room. At one end stood an electric cutting machine which was being deftly operated by a gray-haired man. He was guiding the machine through six-inch thick layers of material and as he worked, oddly-shaped blocks of material fell away and were gathered and stacked systematically, to be later delivered to the proper sewing line. At the other end of the room, irons stood upended on wide ironing tables, their electric cables hanging from the low ceiling and suspended with strings, twine and again, remnants of cloth.

It was hot in the room in spite of the fans whirring overhead. Air conditioning was not introduced in the manufacturing section because it was said that if the labourers became used to the cool of the factory they would not be able to adjust to the heat and humidity of their own homes. They would then not be able to sleep at night and would became inefficient workers during the day.

The steam rising from the ironing table added to the humidity in the room and the men pressing the newly-stitched and freshly washed garments had their shirts clinging damply to their backs. The neatly pressed garments were being slipped into transparent plastic bags under the watchful eyes of the Supervisor, who stood counting the pieces as they were packed into cartons ready for shipment. He always had to be alert and vigilant, otherwise things had a way of disappearing.

The Supervisor, however, was not above turning a blind eye when necessary. If, for instance, he had a visitor at home who brought a plump envelope with him, the next day when the shirts were being counted, the Supervisor might suddenly find the need to make an urgent phone call or answer an equally urgent call of nature. If, on his return, he found a carton or two missing, he would not be terribly perturbed, for a man could not be in several places at once, could he? And anyway, the factory owners made a packet from the labour of poor people like himself. In his opinion a few missing cartons here and there would not only not do them any harm at all, but would also contribute a little to more equitable distribution of wealth.

On her first day at work Mariam was shown how to be a helper, snipping loose thread ends, straightening stitches and keeping things in readiness for the girls working at the machines. Around one o'clock a whistle blew and the single door of the factory floor, which was kept locked to prevent pilferage, was unbolted to let everyone out. Mariam followed the girls to the single toilet which was reserved for women, but the queue was so long that by the time Mariam's turn came lunch period was almost half over.

She joined the other girls who had brought their lunch from home in round two-tiered tiffin carriers. Most of them ate *chapatti* and vegetable curry, the flat unleavened bread and curry being eaten cold as there was no kitchen where they could be reheated. Mariam hurriedly ate her lunch of a plaited bun and a cup of tea bought at the factory canteen and went to see her mother who was waiting outside the factory gates so that they could go to their new home together.

As she approached the padlocked iron gate, Mariam saw a khaki-clad guard run up to her, brandishing a cane. He authoritatively informed her that she could not meet her mother now as no worker was allowed outside the gates until closing time. So Mariam returned to the machine-filled room and, as the guard on the factory floor once again bolted and locked the single door, she could not shake off the claustrophobic feeling of being in some kind of a prison.

Time passed quickly for Mariam and her mother and they settled to their new way of life. She woke up very early every day, seven days a week, and got ready to go to the factory while her mother hurriedly prepared breakfast and some lunch for her to take to work. Like all the other girls, Mariam walked to work although it took more than an hour to get to the factory. But they had little choice because rickshaws were too expensive and there were no cheap transport services to the factory location. In winter the walk was quite pleasant with the sun warming them after a night spent huddled under quilts. But in the monsoons walking could be very difficult when more often than not, they arrived at the factory damp and wet, their umbrellas providing little protection against the torrential rains which sometimes flooded the streets.

The factory was doing very well for everyone said that there were lots of new orders coming in, but as no new hands were being hired, the girls had to put in longer hours of work to meet the extra production. They were all being paid extra wages for the overtime that they were putting in, but for the time being it was only on paper. Their Supervisor assured all the workers that all their overtime dues were being meticulously recorded in the accounts and would be settled during the coming festival. Didn't they agree that it would be much better if everyone got their payments nearer the time of *Eid*, the great Muslim festival which followed Ramadan, the month of fasting and abstinence? Wasn't that the time when one really needed the money for going home to the village, for buying new clothes and for enjoying the holiday season? Of course, the Supervisor neglected to tell the workers that the longer the owners withheld payment the more profit the company made.

Although illiterate, Mariam was an intelligent young woman. Within a few months she had learnt to operate the sewing machines and had graduated from being a helper to actually stitching parts of shirts. Her wages had also increased, but as she paid nearly half her wages for a tiny, cramped room which she shared with her mother, money was still very tight. Resigned for the time being to her new way of life, Mariam sat working at her sewing machine and thought about the large airy room she used to occupy in the brothel and the friendly old man who never raised her room rent. Her present landlady kept demanding higher rent every few months, for small as they were, there was a great demand for these rooms, as more and more girls came from the villages to work at the garment factories in town. Mariam often thought about her quiet Fridays when she chatted with her friends and went to the cinema. Now she was so tired at the end of the day, and so perpetually short of money, that such frivolous expenses as movies were out of the question.

Mariam sighed to herself and thought about her mother alone in their dismal room all day because most of the women in that area went out to work early in the morning and returned late at night. She thought about her present earnings which, even with all her overtime, was only a fraction of what she used to earn as a prostitute. If Mrs. Hashem was right, and Mariam had strong reservations about that, perhaps her soul was being saved but it was hard on her body which seemed to be wearing away very fast. Her mother, too, was unwell and aging rapidly.

She was jolted out of her reverie by a hand that stroked her neck and slid down to squeeze her shoulder before reaching out to inspect the shirt collar held under the needle of her sewing machine. It was the Supervisor. He was a good-looking young man with a light complexion which was highly appreciated at all levels of society. His dark wavy hair complemented his dark eyes, and best of all, he was a bachelor. He was a favourite topic of gossip during the lunch hour, and most of the young girls working in the factory swooned over him, blushing furiously whenever he came up to inspect their work.

"You are very bright and have learnt to do some very specialized stitching in a very short time," said the Supervisor to Mariam. He waited for her to thank him profusely for the praise, beaming and blushing like the other girls. When, saying nothing, she continued to run the sewing machine, he went on, "Under my guidance you can progress even faster you know."

Life having taught her to be practical, Mariam looked up and asked, "How much more wages would I be able to earn?"

"Oh, your salary could double if you manage to graduate to the finishing line. Moreover, while the work is more skilled it's less strenuous so you will not feel so tired all the time. It really is a shame that a beautiful girl like you should have such dark shadows under her eyes."

"But how will I learn the skills that are needed to graduate to the finishing line? I know that those who are there now have been working in the factory for years. At the moment I do not have time even to die. How can I make time to get new training?" asked Mariam, tempted by the promise of an increase in her wages and less time to be spent on the factory floor.

"Don't worry your pretty head about that," the Supervisor comforted her, "Just come to my house after work tonight, and I will explain everything to you."

Having learnt the facts of life the hard way in the brothel, Mariam did not fail to miss the implications of the Supervisor's suggestions. But that did not particularly perturb her. She decided that if this was a shortcut to promotion and higher wages, she saw nothing wrong in it. As a prostitute she used to receive money for her favours, now she could use those same favours to get herself an early promotion. To her mind there was very little difference in the two situations. After all a girl had to use whatever assets she had to progress in this dog-eat-dog world. Didn't she know only too well that there was always a price to be paid for everything that one gained in this life?

After that day Mariam's life, at least financially, became a little easier. Although now she was seldom required to do overtime, she had to report to the Supervisor's house nearly every day after work. He was kind to her and when in a particularly good mood, would take her to wayside food stalls where they would eat barbecued spicy chicken *tikka* and freshly fried *jelabis*, hot and dripping in syrup. Or perhaps they would share a plateful of piquant *chatpatti* with chick peas floating in a rich dark tamarind sauce topped with sliced boiled eggs and chopped green chilies. He usually confined his amorous activities within his room but sometimes, feeling particularly sentimental, he would take her to Ramna Park and, in the shadow of a flowering hibiscus, would make love to her and confide to her all his hopes and dreams for the future. He would usually pay for her rickshaw fare home but it would be nonetheless very late when she would eventually fall asleep at night in her own bed.

Mariam found the new situation tolerable as she was earning more money and could now afford better medical treatment for her mother's illness. She might have continued indefinitely in the new setup if Fate, as she is often wont to do, hadn't decided to take a hand. Her life in the brothel had taught Mariam many ways to avoid pregnancy, and she had been very conscientious about taking all the precautions she knew. Mariam, however, became one of the unfortunate statistics of failure which, in spite of every effort, exist in all things human. Mariam found herself pregnant with the Supervisor's child.

As soon as her pregnancy was confirmed, Mariam went to the Supervisor and told him that she was carrying his child. Mariam was a sensible young woman, fully aware of the lowly station in life in which God in His wisdom had seen fit to place her. She knew better than to bemoan the unfairness of divine decision-making. She therefore did not have even remote expectations of any romantic, emotional or noble gesture on the part of the Supervisor. But in spite of her pragmatic approach, she was unprepared for his irrational outburst.

"How can you be so sure that it is my baby?" shouted the Supervisor. "The owner of the factory himself told me that you were a prostitute. As a favour to Mrs. Hashem, who wanted to rescue you from that filthy life, you had been given the job in the factory. A leopard does not change his spots, you know, and neither does a prostitute change her habits. You must have been moonlighting on the side to add to your wages. A lot of the garment factory girls do that, I know. You can't miss seeing them at night, walking the streets in Gulshan where the foreigners stay. They are all dressed up in bright saris and heavy make-up. God knows it is not cheap living in the city, and I know you have to take care of your sick mother. No, there is no way you can convince me that it is my child and dump the responsibility on my shoulder."

The Supervisor stopped to take a breath and then continued, "But why don't you get rid of it anyway? I am sure from your days in the brothel you must be knowing many midwives or *dais* who do this for a fee."

Her hazel eyes calm and serene, and her angelic face not revealing what she really thought of the Supervisor, Mariam, the complete cynic, replied softly, "Mr. Supervisor, you know very well that you are the only one that I have been seeing. I have been coming to you every day after work because I had agreed to pay your price for my new position in the factory, and everyone in the factory is fully aware of that. People are not blind nor are they fools, you know.

"As for getting rid of the baby, I cannot, and will not do so. You do realize that women like us cannot get married and have husbands who will look after them, that is assuming husbands do look after their wives. Nor can we have children under the usually accepted social setup of marriage and family. This is the first time that I have become pregnant, and I will bring the child into the world because, after all, someone must take care of me in my old age as I am taking care of my mother."

Aware that Mariam was speaking the truth when she claimed him as the father of her child, and knowing well that he would not be able to convince her to have an abortion, the Supervisor fell silent, thinking the matter over. Marrying Mariam was out of the question. His mother had already picked out a young girl for him from his home village and he was due to get married soon. If Mariam continued to work in the factory, her swelling body would be a daily testimony to their relationship, and would make him vulnerable to indiscipline among the workers. No, he had no other choice. Mariam would have to go.

"All right," he said finally, "I will think about it and let me see what I can do."

Next day at work the Supervisor rejected all the shirts that Mariam's had finished, telling her that the quality of her work had fallen far below the required standard. He told her that in recent weeks he had noticed that her performance had been steadily deteriorating, but out of kindness of heart, because he knew that she needed the money for her mother's illness, he had said nothing, hoping that she would improve. In spite of the patience that he had practiced, he found no indications of improvement and so he could not, in all fairness to other workers, allow her any longer to hold her present, well-paid position. If she liked she could go back to sewing seams.

Mariam knew exactly what game the Supervisor was playing. Both knew that she could no longer live on the wages of an ordinary sewing girl. With the baby on the way and her mother's health getting worse day by day, Mariam needed all the money she could earn. She also knew that even if she stubbornly chose to continue working as a sewing girl, the management would lay her off as soon as her pregnant state became apparent, because her tenure at the factory was not long enough to make her eligible for maternity leave, and the terms of her contract did not make her eligible for any other benefits.

In fact, it was a legal loophole used by many garment industries. Women workers were usually contracted for a period which fell just short of qualifying them from becoming eligible for permanent employment and the related benefits. Although many women were aware of this exploitation, they still signed up because the jobs were in great demand, and if they protested too much, the management would have very little trouble in finding replacements.

Brought up in an environment of brothels and prostitutes, Mariam had experienced life in the raw from a very early age. She had long ago found out that to withstand the winds of change in this life, one must be cynical, philosophical, and skim life at a superficial level. To drink deeply of such a life was only to expose oneself to pain so excruciating as to turn one insane. One accepted the games that Fate played for there was little else to be done.

But in her own heart Mariam felt that she held a trump card. For was it not said that on Judgement Day Allah was bound to answer all questions on life and its meaning? On that day, Mariam vowed, she would challenge the Almighty. He would have to explain to her why when she sold her body for giving pleasure she was considered a sinner, but when she sold her health for making rich people richer, it was considered an honourable profession. She had played the game of life to the best of her ability with whatever hand had been dealt her. For the rest Allah was responsible — Allah, the Merciful and the Benevolent.

So Mariam packed her bags, and together with her mother, returned to the old man's house. The old man was sitting in his courtyard with his foot on a stool. A little boy was massaging his head and the old man was half asleep in relaxed pleasure. When Mariam greeted him he opened his eyes sleepily and called her to sit by him. He was genuinely happy to see her for he had always found Mariam very special and different from the type of women who usually rented his rooms. Patting her kindly on the head, and nodding sagely, he observed, "I knew you would return. Prostitutes can never live any other kind of life. They always come back."

Mariam was quite fond of the old man, so she smiled and said nothing. What was there to say anyway? Who would be interested in listening to her sad and miserable story? A prostitute's job was to supply pleasure, and for a short while, make a man forget his own troubles. No one was interested in getting burdened with her sorrows.

Everyone felt that they had more than their own share already. And perhaps the old man and the Supervisor were right. Leopards cannot change their spots, and prostitutes cannot change their habits.

So she smiled and asked how everyone was in the building. She learnt that Mrs. Hashem continued to make regular visits to the brothel and give long lectures to the old man as well as the women on their disgraceful way of life. And in the course of this conversation Mariam was inordinately pleased to find that her old room in the corner of the house had just been vacated. Mrs. Hashem had managed to persuade yet another young prostitute to save her soul and look for another profession.

THE MATCHMAKER[1]

It was just after the dawn *azaan*, the call for the first of the five daily prayers mandatory for the followers of Islam. For Rokeya it was the nicest time of the day. The sky only faintly light and the air still cool before the sun's heat sucked it all away. You could smell the earth damp with the night's dew, and you could hear the rustling and the stirring of the birds making ready to fly out at first light. But the cuckoo was already up and about, filling the air with its disconsolate cry, urgently seeking for who knew what.

Rokeya stretched pleasurably and took up the spiky broom made from the spines of dried coconut fronds and prepared to sweep the hard, mud-packed courtyard. Dry leaves drifting down from the many trees surrounding the little homestead littered the yard, mingling with stray bits of straw and chicken droppings. She bent from the waist down and, tossing her thick, black, oiled and braided hair over her shoulder, started to sweep methodically around the yard. She collected the debris, threw it into the undergrowth and stood the broom in its usual corner by the chicken coop. Then she lifted the large dome-shaped cover made of latticed bamboo which housed the ducks and chickens during the night. The birds bustled out, indignant at being cooped in for so long, and made for the corner of the yard where Rokeya and her mother usually cleaned the rice, separating the grains from husks and small pebbles, by tossing the rice in horseshoe-shaped trays made from the ubiquitous bamboo. A cock crowed from somewhere nearby, and a cow lowed plaintively, anxious to be milked.

In a little shed at the side of the house, Rokeya started the fire in the *chula* and made a mental note that the next time she mud-plastered the courtyard, she should also plaster the earthen stove, as cracks had begun to appear at its sides. As she put the old tin kettle on for making tea, the household began to stir. Rokeya's father, Rafiq Mia, came out yawning, a green and red checkered cotton gamcha on his shoulder. He sat near the *chula* on a *piri* waiting for his morning cup of tea. The low slab of wood which served for a seat was raised only a few inches off the floor, and Rafiq sat with his knees drawn nearly to his chin. Rokeya's mother Amena, soon emerged, and taking the cup of tea that Rokeya had prepared, handed it to her husband, together with a shallow earthen bowl filled with puffed rice with a small piece of crystallized molasses sitting on top like a crown. Rafiq ate and drank in silence. Then tying the *gamcha* round his waist, he picked up his basket and shovel and disappeared round the corner of the house, brushing against the softly nodding leaves of the *kakrol* vine climbing along the mud walls of the little house. Rokeya's father was a day labourer and he had to get to the marketplace early to ensure that he got hired for a full day's work.

Rokeya quickly doused the fire because the leaves and twigs gathered from the nearby mango orchard must be made to last. Besides, no one else except her father was allowed to take tea. It was too expensive. By now, Rokeya's three younger brothers had come out rubbing their eyes and demanding to be fed. They were each given a handful of puffed rice and a bowl of water from the earthen pitcher standing in a shady corner of the courtyard. The squat black pitcher, its mouth covered with the empty shell of half a coconut, kept the water cool and sweet even on the hottest of days.

Rokeya and her mother drank just water and prepared for the day's work. They would eat later when Rafiq came home with rice and some vegetables purchased from his day's wages. In the meantime, there was plenty of other chores to be done. The water had to be fetched from the pond a mile or so away, leaves and twigs had to be collected, and if there was time, Amena would take the boys to the flooded paddy fields to trap some small fish which would add some flavour to tonight's dinner, which as usual would be meager.

Rokeya was thirteen and too old to go wading in paddy fields. She would stay at home and apply a mixture of clay and water to the courtyard which had begun to crack in places and was raising a lot of dust in the slightest of breeze. Later she would walk to the nearby field where cows usually grazed, and pick up pats of cow dung. She would mix the dung with bits of straw to make flat round cakes. These she would stick to the west-facing wall of the house, which remained sun-drenched for the better part of the day. In a day or two, the crisp brown dung cakes with the four finger marks making ridges down the middle, would be stored for use as fuel. If she was lucky, she would be able to pluck a stray guava or two from trees dotting the fields. These would help to fill her stomach for she was always hungry and found it hard waiting so long for her first meal of the day.

As the sun reached the top of the heavens and the heat became intense, her father returned home. On the way he had stopped at the local marketplace and had bought some rice and a bundle of jute leaves. Dumping the old shopping bag on the porch, he went off to the pond to bathe. Rokeya hurriedly lit the fire and set the rice to boil. Her mother stripped the leaves from the long stalks in preparation for cooking. She plucked two young *kakrols* from the vine and, after discarding the hard, flat seeds, sliced the prickly, yellow-green vegetables to add to the curry. By the time her father returned from his bath, the simple meal was ready. The three boys sat down with their father to eat the freshly boiled rice and steamed vegetables flavoured with dry red chilly which had been charred black in the ashes of the wood fire.

Amena sat fanning her husband while he ate. When the meal was over, Rokeya rolled out the straw mat under the shade of the mango tree for her father to lie down and sleep. She and her mother were then free to go and bathe at the pond. They each owned only two sets of clothes — the one they were wearing and the one they carried with them. At the pond, they bathed and washed their clothes, and then hung them out to dry on a rope strung between two old papaya trees at the back of the house. They finally sat down to eat. Although very hungry, they ate sparingly, leaving enough for an evening meal for Rokeya's father and her three brothers.

The call for the afternoon prayers came wafting over the breeze. Wiping his face with his *gamcha* after performing the customary ablutions in preparation for prayers, Rokeya's father made his way to the little whitewashed village mosque. On his return he had the village matchmaker with him.

The matchmaker was a small, bent old man, wearing once-white pajamas and a loose, collarless shirt with a rim of grime round the neck. The rubber pumps on his feet were dusty and worn, and his black umbrella, which he now carried folded under his sweat-stained arm, had faded to a light gray. To Rafiq and his wife, however, he was an honoured guest. There was a daughter of marriageable age in the house, and who else could inform them of eligible boys but the matchmaker? For that was exactly what the matchmaker did. He wandered round villages, gossiped with all and sundry, became a storehouse of information and acted as a veritable one-man marriage bureau.

When Rafiq announced the visitor to his wife, she hurried out of the house to proffer the matchmaker the special guest mat and the pungent, aromatic *paan* leaves which her husband was in the habit of chewing when relaxing after the day's backbreaking work. The matchmaker sat down with a sigh on the mat and delicately pushed the betel-leaf cone stuffed with diced betelnut, katechu and lime, into his cheek. Chewing contentedly, he spat red spittle into a corner of the yard. The white lime on his fingers he wiped on the walls of the house which bore signs of having being used for this purpose by others as well.

Satisfied that he had been given the honour and respect that he deserved, the matchmaker leaned forward and in hushed tones whispered that he had a marriage proposal for their daughter. The younger son of a farmer from a neighboring village was of marriageable age. True, the boy did not have a proper job because the land that the family owned was too small for even the father and the elder son to work on. But still, the boy had potential because he had applied for a job as a labourer in the Middle East and was waiting to hear from a distant relative who lived in the capital, and who had promised to help the boy in the matter. The family had even sold a cow and a part of their homestead to raise the money which the relative said would be needed to make all the arrangements. Furthermore, the matchmaker went on persuasively, their dowry demands were very reasonable. They wanted only a bicycle and a wristwatch for the groom. Considering that the boy's future was assured, the matchmaker argued, surely these demands were nothing. Anyone else would have asked the bride's father to pay all the expenses for the boy's overseas travel.

Rafiq could sell off the bamboo grove behind the house and that bit of land on the other side of the river to pay for the watch and the bicycle, the matchmaker suggested to Rokeya's father, for everyone knew who owned what in the village. Rokeya was his only daughter and Rafiq would not have to worry about his three sons Allah had blessed him with. In fact, they would bring wealth to the family when they got married. So there was really nothing for Rokeya's father to worry about.

In fact, it was lucky for Rafiq that he, the matchmaker, had found such an ideal match before people started commenting about a grown girl like Rokeya still remaining unmarried. And what a match. A God-given match. The matchmaker raised his hands heavenward and invoked Allah's blessing for such an auspicious act.

Then he coughed and murmured, "I do not want to mention such matters at this stage, Rafiq Mia, but please keep in mind that a matchmaker must be paid a small fee for his services. But for such a happy occasion, it is indeed a small price to pay."

"If Allah's will be done, then it goes without saying that we will pay you well for the great favour you are doing us," Rokeya's father assured the matchmaker.

Then turning to his wife, Rafiq Mia asked "Well, what do you think, Rokeya's Ma?"

In the village it is traditional to address a married woman as the mother of her first born, with the result that over the years the woman's given name is often forgotten by almost everyone. Amena also addressed Rafiq as the father of her firstborn, not only as a mark of respect, but also because it was considered unlucky to address one's husband by name. This custom, which has over time taken superstitious overtones, has its roots in the ancient Arab practice of conferring on men and women the title of father or mother of their first born as a mark of respect. This same tradition has endured since Islam was first introduced in Bengal in the thirteenth century.

Rokeya's mother, sitting just inside the doorway of the house so that she could follow the conversation without being fully exposed to the visitor, adjusted the sari that covered her head and said, "What can I say, Rokeya's Father? The matchmaker is a respected elder of the village. He has all our interests at heart. He knows how anxious we are to marry off Rokeya as soon as possible. And if the boy finds work in foreign countries, then my Rokeya will at least be well fed. I have nothing more to say. It is upto Allah and to you."

So the matchmaker was paid his not-so-small fee, and Rokeya was married in a red and gold sari which had been bought specially from town. She wore flowers in her hair, glass bangles tinkled on her wrists, and red and gold sandals adorned her feet. Her face was outlined with little white dots made from sandalwood paste, the line ending in a curl on each cheek. Between her nostrils, nestling in the hollow above her lips, hung a little silver nose ring. The groom was dressed in white pajamas, which clung, tightly to his calves, a high-necked, gold lurex coat, which hung to his knees, and a white turban on his head. All through the wedding ceremony, as was expected of any self-respecting groom from a good family, he decorously held a white, folded handkerchief to his mouth.

After the wedding dinner of fragrant *pulao* and beef curry had been consumed, the individual little earthen plates licked clean of the sweet *firni* made from ground rice and thickened milk, and *paan* stuffed with herbs and shredded coconut distributed among the guests, it was time for the bride to take leave of her father's home. Rokeya was helped into a rickshaw which had been curtained all around with an old sari to shield her from vulgar stares. With her new husband walking alongside her rickshaw, Rokeya was borne away to her in-laws home which, if she was a good daughter-in-law and wife, as her grandmother had told her so many times, she would leave only in the funereal cot.

For Rokeya life did not change a great deal. She still got up at the first call for dawn prayers, only now she swept her father-in-law's courtyard instead of her father's. She then washed the pots and pans and fed the men folk. Rokeya had not seen any other way of life in her own parents' home and, not expecting anything else from her new life, was neither disappointed nor unhappy. In fact she quite admired her young husband who was strong and had bold black eyes. He did not stay at home much, but then in her experience, men never did. Women had their place in the home and men outside. It was the will of Allah as she had been taught from childhood.

One day, about a month after the wedding, Rokeya's husband came storming home. He had just received news that the relative in the capital had absconded with the money given him for arranging her husband's job abroad. No one knew where the relative had gone. Some said that he had used the money to find himself a job overseas. Some said that he had stolen the money and was hiding in another town until the excitement died down. Rokeya's husband tore at his hair and screamed and shouted. His life was ended, his future bleak. Who could have guessed that the relative would turn out to be such a traitor?

Rokeya's mother-in-law wailed day and night. Her cow gone, her land gone, and all for nothing. It was all Rokeya's fault. She was the one with the bad luck. She was jinxed. Disaster of this magnitude had not struck the family until Rokeya entered the household. No such calamity had befallen them till now. Why on earth did she agree to bring in a daughter-in-law from such a lowly family as a day labourer's? The dowry Rokeya had brought was a pittance. Rokeya was responsible for ruining her husband's life. Why did she not burn in hell?

Bewildered, Rokeya could not understand what she had done to bring such ill luck to the family. She began to believe that she must have been born under ill-omened stars. She began to believe that it was her duty to turn the tidal wave of disaster. But how does a thirteen-year old girl do that?

Within her limited experience, Rokeya did what she could. She tried to placate her mother-in-law by asking forgiveness for she knew not what crime. Day and night she cried rivers of tears and massaged her mother-in-law's head and feet with warm oil in an attempt to assuage her anger. She cooked and cleaned and took over all the backbreaking jobs in the household.

But nothing pacified mother and son. They took up a new refrain. The only way that Rokeya could win forgiveness for being such an ill-fated daughter-in-law and wife, was by bringing money from her father so that her husband could go abroad. Rokeya was thunderstruck. She knew her father had sold his last resources to meet her husband's dowry demands. She tried to explain as much to her in-laws. They paid little heed. They accused her father of having given a cheap watch and an old bicycle which had hardly fetched anything when her husband had sold them at the weekly market held in the village green. In fact, they had fetched barely enough to pay for her son's drinks and gambling debts, her mother-in-law sneered.

And since Rokeya was the harbinger of bad luck, she could not and would not be allowed to stay in the house a day longer. She must return to her father's home immediately and, only when her father had provided for his son-in-law's expenses for going overseas, could Rokeya contemplate returning to her husband's home.

But Rokeya knew that the only way her father could raise that kind of money was by selling the homestead. But that was unthinkable for then where would her father, mother and brothers live? Rokeya also knew that she could not stand up to her in-laws. That she was powerless to prevent them from sending her back to her father's home in disgrace.

That very night Rokeya made a journey which was very different from the one she had made only a few weeks ago on her wedding day. Accompanied by her husband who had borrowed a bicycle for the occasion, and with only the dim headlamp lighting the way, Rokeya was made to walk the long way back to her village.

At first her parents were overjoyed to see them both, thinking that this was an unexpected visit by the newly-married couple. The delusions, however, were soon shattered, when her husband began to accuse her father for having palmed off an ill-fated daughter on him. As her husband started to scream his demands for money at her father, Rokeya hung her head lower and lower in shame, praying that the ground would open up and swallow her whole, so that she would not have to witness her father's humiliation for which she alone was responsible.

At first Rafiq tried to pacify his hysterical son-in-law. When that failed, he pleaded with his son-in-law to take Rokeya back while he, Rafiq, tried to raise the money. Bringing Rokeya to her father's house in disgrace only a month after the wedding was a dishonour for the whole family, and would leave a terrible mark on her. Rafiq and his wife would not be able to lift up their heads and meet the eyes of the villagers. Rokeya would become a social outcast. Rafiq laid his *gamcha* over his open palms like a beggar and beseeched his son-in-law to take Rokeya back with him.

But all to no avail. Rokeya's husband was adamant. If he took Rokeya back, he argued, Rafiq would never raise the money he needed. If he wanted his daughter to be able to raise her head in good society, then Rafiq had better do something quickly about fulfilling his son-in-law's demands.

Back in her father's home, Rokeya still got up at the first call of morning prayers but she no longer found any pleasure in the early morning breeze, the dew-soaked trees and the chirps and rustles of the sleepy birds. As before she swept the courtyard and let out the chickens and ducks, but now had to face the unbearable situation where she was unwanted in her in-law's house and was being tolerated in her own parents' home. Her presence in her father's house was a heavy burden for her parents to bear. The fact that it was not Rokeya's fault did not help to ease matters for anyone, for there was even less to eat in the house than before. Before her marriage, the sale of an occasional bamboo from the grove behind the house, helped cover expenses when times were hard. Now even the bamboo was gone.

Rokeya could not understand why she felt so guilty about everything that had happened. She could not understand why she felt convinced that, in some way, it really was all her fault.

"But I always did what I was told by my elders," she argued to herself. "Grandma told me that if I obeyed my elders and did not complain about my situation in life, Allah would be pleased with me and I would achieve happiness and bring happiness to others. But Grandma was wrong. I tried to keep everyone happy, accepted whatever came my way, and still no one is happy — not my husband, not my in-laws, not my own parents, and least of all me. I don't seem to fit in anywhere. My parents can't feed me and my husband wants money more than he wants me. There does not seem to be any place or need for me in this world."

She began to believe that perhaps her husband was right and that she was an omen of ill fortune and that perhaps her mother-in-law was not wrong when she repeatedly shrieked day and night that Rokeya would bring bad luck to whoever had the misfortune to be associated with her.

That night the moon rose round and full. The night was so bright that some confused crows began to flap their wings and caw in the false light, thinking that morning had already dawned. The howl of a lone jackal came over the still night air, and somewhere nearby, an owl hooted in reply. Frogs droned in the little ditch by the wayside, lulling those who were still awake into a state of somnambulance.

But for Rokeya there was no sleep. She got up from the floor where she was lying next to her baby brother and stepped through the doorway into the little courtyard which she had freshly swept that evening. She looked at the orange-gold moon through the leaves of the mango tree and sighed a deep, deep sigh.

At the first call for morning prayers, they found her dead body swinging from the mango tree in the early morning breeze. A cuckoo was calling frantically in the bamboo grove.

That afternoon, just after the *asar* prayers, the matchmaker, his faded black umbrella shielding his balding head from the sun, padded his way to the next village. He met the father of a girl who was eighteen years old but was still unmarried because she had a limp in her right leg.

The matchmaker said, "I have news of a wonderful boy. Unfortunately, his family was cheated out of the money given to a relative to make the necessary arrangements for the boy to work abroad as a labourer. We all know that your daughter is defective, that she cannot walk straight. If you can raise the money for the boy's passage, I can persuade his family to agree to the marriage in spite of your daughter's limp. There will, of course, be a small fee for services rendered."

The grateful father warmly shook the matchmaker's hand and ushered him into his house, calling to his wife to bring out the guest mat and a plate of *paan*.

---

[1] The story was first published in *Selected Short Stories from Bangladesh*, UPL, 1998.

THE GOAT

Rabeya straightened her back and with the end of her well-patched sari, wiped the sweat running in rivulets from her forehead down her neck. She had just finished ploughing the field, and although it was no more than the size of a pocket handkerchief, she was exhausted. Her day had started with the call for the morning prayer. She had got up, careful not to wake Khalil, her invalid husband, and Moyna, her four-year old daughter.

Mercifully the community tubewell was near her house. She pumped hard on the iron handle, and after the third push, the water came gushing out in torrents. It took but a few minutes to fill her two pitchers with clear, clean underground water. But she had to get up early to fetch the water, as otherwise there would be a long queue at the water pump, and she had a lot of work to do. With expertise born of long practice, she balanced one of the pitchers on her head and the other on her hips, and walked the short distance home.

She stood one of the pitchers in the corner of the tiny mudpacked courtyard of her house, in readiness for her husband to wash his hands and face as Khalil was too weak to work the pump. The other she placed in the little covered area which served as her kitchen, reserving the water for drinking and cooking. She had already performed the ritual ablutions at the well, and now, facing west, she spread the straw mat on the ground, and quickly said the brief morning prayers. She then started the fire with dry leaves and twigs, to make tea for her husband.

She knew he was awake because she could hear him cough and wheeze, trying to clear the phlegm which always collected in his chest overnight. It had happened quite suddenly. One day last year, Khalil had returned home from a day spent in cutting earth for a road that was being built just outside their village. He had collapsed on the floor, his body wracked by fits of coughing, until Rabeya was terrified that he would die right there and then. She had run to the herbalist who lived close by the mosque, and he had given her some dark powder telling her to mix it with clean water and feed it to her husband every time he had a coughing attack. Miraculously, the mixture had soothed his cough, but he remained too weak and incapacitated to do any work. All he could do was lean against the doorpost and stare into the distance, disaster reflected in his eyes.

And well he may despair, because Khalil had no other livelihood but to sell his labour. The rice from the tiny plot of land, which he had inherited as his share when his father had died, barely filled his family's stomach for two months of the year. For the rest of the time Khalil had to find manual labour, while Rabeya stayed home to cook, clean and wash, fetch the water, collect firewood, weed and tend the land, and take care of Moyna. To add some flavour to their daily meal of rice and lentils, Rabeya also grew some vegetable vines which climbed along the walls of her house and spread greenly on the thatched roof, providing a little extra protection from the hot sun. She kept two chickens which survived on whatever they could scratch from the earth around the house. Rabeya sometimes sold an egg or two in the market, but usually reserved them for Khalil who needed good food to keep up his energy.

During harvest time, Rabeya also worked in the village headman's house as he owned several plots of land from which he cropped vast quantities of paddy. Rabeya helped to husk, winnow, parboil and dry the rice, which were then stored in great earthen vats securely ensconced in the mudpacked floor of the headman's house. For this work Rabeya received rice or paddy.

Khalil and Rabeya had been married less than five years, and had so far managed to maintain a delicate balance between starvation and survival, but when Khalil fell ill, this fragile stability tilted precariously towards disaster. Khalil had neither the strength nor the money to visit a doctor in town which was a rickshaw and a bus ride away, and none of the village doctors could pinpoint what was really wrong with him. So Khalil drank the herbal potion when his cough was particularly bad, and prayed to Allah that he would be cured so that he could take care of his family.

In the meantime they had to find ways and means to stay alive.

"Moyna's mother," Khalil called Rabeya one morning, " It is time to prepare the land for planting, and there is no one but you to do it."

"But what will people say, Moyna's father?" queried Rabeya, "You know women are not supposed to plough the land. It is said to bring bad luck."

"My dear wife," sighed Khalil, "We either starve or risk the bad luck. Anyway our luck could not really get worse than it already is, can it? So go to Old Man Hakim tomorrow and see if he will rent us his cow and his plough. His cow is sickly and his plough blunt, but this is all we can afford. And tell him we will pay him at harvest time."

So Rabeya paid a visit to Old Man Hakim and fetched his cow and ploughshare. She had to rest twice on the way back because the ploughshare was heavy and she had to carry it on her shoulder all the way. So here she was trying to prepare this patch of land with a cow that was as feeble as her husband, and a ploughshare that barely broke the soil. She straightened her aching back and stared despondently at the result of her several days' hard work. The fruit of her labour was heart-breakingly disappointing.

As darkness fell, she tethered the cow in her courtyard and fed it some leaves and grass which she had collected on her way home from the field. She stood the plough in a corner and started preparing the evening meal. As she sat stirring the bubbling pot of rice, Rabeya thought to herself, "Tomorrow is Friday, market day, I could sell the six eggs I have saved, and buy some oil and spices. And, oh yes, the gourd on the roof is ready for plucking. I will use that to pay the herbal doctor for Moyna's father's medicine." Even in her thoughts,

Rabeya would not dream of addressing her husband by name as to do so would bring bad luck.

Next morning, after attending to her husband's needs, Rabeya tied the eggs in a loose bundle at her waist, and taking her daughter with her, hurried to the *haat* which was held every Friday at the village green. It was early, and people were still setting out their wares. Here the vegetable vendor was arranging potatoes, onions and eggplants in pyramids, there the cloth merchant was hanging out checkered *lungis* for men, and brightly patterned cotton saris for women. The gypsies would come a little later with baskets of multicoloured glass bangles twinkling in the bright sunlight.

Rabeya found some discarded hay, arranged the eggs in a nest and waited for customers. Soon she spied her friend, Halima, who was carrying some chickens. The birds, feet tied, and swinging upside down from her hands, loudly protested their discomfort. Rabeya made Moyna sit guard over the eggs while she went over to chat with her friend.

"You are selling three chickens today, Halima, and only last week you sold a young goat. How are you managing to do so well?" asked Rabeya, not bothering to hide the envy in her voice.

Halima laughed. "If you had any time to spare after taking care of your invalid husband, your work at the headman's house and your home, then you too could be doing something that earned you real money."

"Don't I know it," sighed Rabeya, "On top of everything else, I now have to plough the land and plant seedlings. Last night I could not sleep from the aches and pains in my body, and Khalil made it worse, coughing throughout the night. Every day it is becoming more and more difficult to cope with my problems."

"I don't think you should try to farm the land yourself," advised Halima. "Even if your piece of land is small, you are already burdened with too much work. This will ruin your health. And then who will take care of little Moyna and her father? Why don't you sharecrop it out? You know you can get half of what will be produced."

Halima turned away to haggle with a potential buyer while Rabeya pondered over what she had said. It was true that she alone was keeping the family alive, and if she became ill then they would all become destitute and reduced to begging in the streets of the nearest town.

"What you say is right, Halima," said Rabeya finally. "I will ask Shafi Mia who owns the plot next to ours, if he would lease it from us for sharecropping."

"Oh, by the way," said Halima, tying the money she got from selling her chickens in a tight knot at the end of her sari and tucking it into her waist, "If you can find the time, come to my house tomorrow morning. The women who belong to my group are holding the regular weekly meeting and it will help you to understand how I am able to sell goats one week and chickens the next!" And Halima bustled off, satisfied with her day's transactions at the market.

Feeling distinctly less despondent than when she had come to the market, Rabeya sold off her eggs, bought some soya bean oil and turmeric, and thoughtfully returned home. Maybe, just maybe, Allah was showing her a way to solve her insurmountable problems.

Soon after that day, things began to look up for Rabeya. She returned the cow and ploughshare to Old Man Hakim and promised to bring round some eggs and vegetables in lieu of the hire charge. She then paid a visit to Shafi Mia. It was late evening, and she found him sitting in his courtyard smoking contentedly on a hand-held *hookah*.

"What brings you here, Moyna's *Ma*?" asked Shafi Mia. "I trust all is well with your husband and daughter."

"They are as well as can be expected in our situation, Brother Shafi," replied Rabeya. Although they were not related, custom dictated that she address Shafi Mia as a respected elder brother. "It is time to prepare the land and plant the seedlings. But although our plot of land is small, with all my other work I cannot do the farming. So Moyna's Father has sent me to ask you if you would be interested in sharecropping our land."

Shafi Mia had been waiting for this day for a long time. Even when Khalil's father was alive, Shafi Mia had been interested in acquiring that particular plot because although it was small it was very good land, and he already owned most of the land around it. He had offered to buy it once, but Khalil's father had refused to part with it, saying that he wanted to leave his sons some assets, however little it might be. After Khalil's father died, Shafi Mia did not try to make any offer to Khalil himself, because he knew that only in very dire circumstances would a man part with his inherited land. So he had bided his time and it seemed that his patience had been rewarded. True, Khalil was not offering to sell the land but only to sharecrop it, but there were ways and means to force a man's hand, and Shafi Mia was a past master at the art, or else how did he become the owner of so much land?

Concealing his interest, Shafi Mia made as if to think deeply on the matter and said, "It is already a little late for the planting, but I can see that your situation is desperate, and since you call me elder brother, it is my duty to help you. So I will sharecrop it for you this season on a fifty-fifty basis."

Relieved that the matter had been settled so easily, Rabeya turned her attention to other matters and, under Halima's tutelage and guidance, she joined a women's group.

Rabeya's life fell into a pattern. She cooked, cleaned and looked after her family, and once a week met with the other members of her group. The social organization which was working with the village women sent a trainer to teach them how to form a group and work together. The trainer warned the women that the group had to prove that its intentions were serious by first setting up a savings fund to which every member made equal contribution. The amount should be what everyone could afford, and they should also set a rate of interest which was acceptable to all. If the group managed to stay together and successfully operate the savings fund for at least six months, the organization would help it to get loans from the bank for whatever work the members decided to do. To help them become a strong and cohesive body, the trainer encouraged them to discuss their problems at the regular weekly meetings and to help one another find solutions.

Rabeya's group consisted of five women whom she had known since she had moved to the village after her marriage to Khalil. To raise the money for her contribution to the savings fund, Rabeya sold some eggs and a papaya from the tree at the back of her house. She was overjoyed when all the members in her group agreed that Rabeya was the most needy amongst them and voted that she get the first loan from the group's savings fund. The only condition was that Rabeya would have to repay her loan and interest within one year. Since the interest rate was far less than what any of the village money lenders would have charged, Rabeya was confident that she would be able to repay her loan in full when the time came.

Rabeya used her very modest loan to buy some paddy which she parboiled and husked and then resold at the market. Her profit was small, but she gained some side benefits because she could use the chaff as feed for her chickens and they laid eggs more frequently. She managed her money well, and long before the year was over, Rabeya had not only repaid her loan in full, but had also generated a small capital of her own.

In the meantime, she also regularly visited their plot of land to keep track of Shafi Mia's activities. He had chosen to cultivate jute, and she was pleased to see the stalks rising straight and tall, the small green leaves quivering in the breeze. Just looking at the jute plants it was difficult to imagine that they could produce such beautiful strands of golden fibre. She knew that when the plants matured, they would be cut down and the stalks soaked in water for several days before the long, thick threads could be extracted. The shining skeins would then be laid out to dry by roadsides, on hedges and in courtyards, before being tied in bales and transported by headload to the market for sale. Rabeya was aware that jute was used to make gunny sacks because these were used extensively in the village, but she had no idea that in towns and cities people used carpets, and even textiles, made from this wonderful flaxen fibre.

On her way home, Rabeya met Shafi Mia going to the mosque for the evening prayers and asked him when harvesting would begin. She was delighted to hear him reply, "Soon, it will be soon. It has been perfect weather for jute and, Allah be praised, the price in the market is better than ever. Allah willing we will make good money this year. My decision to grow jute was the right one."

Happy at the prospect of having some of her financial problems solved, Rabeya was already planning to use their share of the profits to buy some proper medicine for Khalil which would cure his strange affliction. In the meantime, her group had proved itself to be stable and had secured a bank loan. The members had once more unanimously voted that Rabeya was not only in the greatest need of the loan, but that she had also proved herself highly efficient and trustworthy for, had she not returned her loan from the group's savings fund in less than six months?

The loan this time was quite substantial. So Rabeya went into the nearby town and bought packets of sweet and salted biscuits, cigarettes, and small bags of sweets. Every day she helped Khalil settle on a gunny sack at the crossroads near the village green with the wares spread before him. Since it did not demand anything more than sitting and selling the goods, Khalil easily managed the work and was happy to be productive once more. The location was a good one, and people frequently stopped to buy biscuits or smoke a cigarette and chat with Khalil. Soon they began to suggest that Khalil should also sell tea because biscuits were too dry by themselves. Happily Khalil promised that, Allah willing, as soon as they had paid back their bank loan, they would take out a bigger one and start a tea stall where they would place a nice wooden bench for people to sit, drink tea and pass the time of day.

Then one day the even keel of Rabeya's life was once again disturbed. On one of her regular visits to their plot of land, Rabeya found that the harvesting had been done and the jute stalks all cut and taken away. Nothing remained but stubble. Shocked, she at first consoled herself, "Shafi Mia perhaps did not find me at home and so could not let me know that he was about to do the harvesting."

She made her way to Shafi Mia's house and met him just as he was about to enter the mosque.

"Brother Shafi," said Rabeya, "I see you have harvested the jute from our plot. When can I come to collect our share of the profits?"

"Later, later," said Shafi Mia, and adjusting the white crocheted cap so that it sat snugly on his head, he hurried into the mosque to join the congregation for the evening prayers.

"I will come back tomorrow morning, Brother," Rabeya called out to him. "Please keep the money ready. I need it very badly for Moyna's father's treatment and medicine."

"Yes, yes," said Shafi Mia gruffly, "I'll see what I can do."

Early next morning Rabeya went to Shafi Mia's house where his wife told her to wait as Shafi Mia was taking his bath. So Rabeya squatted in a corner of the courtyard, feeling a little annoyed at all the delay.

"These big farmers think we poor people have nothing else to do but wait around all day at their beck and call," Rabeya thought angrily, as the waiting stretched to two hours.

"If I were in Shafi Mia's place, I would give a poor woman like myself her share of the money as soon as possible. After all, I haven't come begging for alms. We have a business deal and Shafi Mia should respect that. He goes to the mosque five times a day to pray, but look at how he treats a poor woman," grumbled Rabeya to herself as the waiting stretched to three hours.

Finally Shafi Mia's wife came out and counted out some money to Rabeya.

"But Sister-in-law," said Rabeya, using that term of address because she called Shafi Mia elder brother. "There is some mistake. When I went into town to buy biscuits and cigarettes, I found out the price at which jute is being sold this year. I should be getting twice the amount that you have given me."

"I don't know what the agreement was between you, but your brother says that this is what he owes you," said Shafi Mia's wife.

Rabeya did not know it, but this was all a part of Shafi Mia's tactics to take away the little plot of land. First, the long wait to create greater urgency for the cash. Then, Rabeya would be in so much need of money, that she would readily accept whatever he was offering her. A few such manoeuvres, and Khalil would be forced to sell his land. Shafi Mia was powerful enough to stop Khalil from leasing or selling the land to anyone else. Shafi Mia would make sure that he was there to grab it at first opportunity and at the cheapest price.

A few months ago these tactics, and Shafi Mia's wealth, would have intimidated Rabeya into accepting what had been offered. She would have returned home frustrated and angry, but impotent to fight the injustice being committed by the rich against the poor. But now Rabeya felt different. She was not wholly dependent on that piece of land and could withstand the pressure for a few days. She had the women's group behind her, and hadn't they all pledged to help each other in times of trouble? Now was the time to test how strong and cohesive the group really was.

Gaining moral strength from these reflections, Rabeya said, "Sister-in-law, Shafi Brother is not keeping to the terms of the agreement and I cannot accept the payment you are offering me."

Shafi Mia's wife shrugged and said, "Suit yourself. It is your choice, but don't you think it is better to have a one-eyed uncle than to have none at all? I should take whatever you are getting now because later you might not get even that."

"I only want what is owing to me. I am not asking for charity and it is not right that rich people like you should take advantage of a poor woman like me. I will approach the village elders about this," said Rabeya, more confidently than she felt, because she knew well that village elders, more often that not, tended to side with the rich and the powerful. Perhaps Shafi Mia's wife was right. She should take what she was getting now, in case she lost everything later. Finally, in spite of her misgivings, and banking on support from her group, Rabeya walked away without accepting the payment.

Next day, Rabeya called a meeting of her group members and told them the whole story of how she had leased Khalil's little plot of land to Shafi Mia for sharecropping, and how the rich farmer was now trying to cheat them out of their full share of the profits. She told her group that Shafi Mia thought them to be very weak, not only because were they poor, but also because Khalil was an invalid and she a mere woman.

The women's group realized that these were ploys to further weaken Rabeya's financial condition so that in the near future she would be forced to sell the piece of land to avoid starvation. This was not the first time that such tactics have been used, nor would it be the last. But this time, with their new-found solidarity, the women decided to fight back. They would go as group to Shafi Mia and demand Rabeya's rightful share on her behalf so that he realized that she was not alone, but had the support of others.

Shafi Mia, however, had been forewarned by some of his hired hands. When he caught sight of the little group approaching his house, he slipped out the back door. He had no intention of facing the wrath of five irate women. So when Rabeya and her friends, excited and talking loudly amongst themselves, arrived at Shafi Mia's house, they were brought up short, because there was no one to whom they could make their demands. The front door was padlocked, for Shafi Mia's wife had only that morning gone to pay a long overdue visit to her brother in the next village.

Thwarted and not knowing what to do next, the dispirited women turned to leave, when they saw a goat tethered in the courtyard placidly feeding on glossy round leaves of the jackfruit tree. She was a handsome animal, with a big round belly that announced her imminent motherhood. Everyone in the village knew that she was Shafi Mia's great pride and that he had paid a hefty price for her in the cattle market that was held twice a year in a village ten miles away. She was a special mixed breed, the likes of which no one had seen before in the village. Shafi Mia expected to make good money from selling her kids in the near future.

Their frustration turning to triumph, the women decided to confiscate the goat to force Shafi Mia to pay Rabeya her dues. The animal was tied with a piece of rope to a wooden peg staked into the earth. The women uprooted the peg and led the goat away, the animal bleating her protest at being wrenched from her succulent meal.

It didn't take very long for everyone in the village to know what Rabeya and her friends had done and why. Soon Shafi Mia became the laughing stock of the village and the brunt of many jokes. It was difficult for him to go anywhere without hearing disparaging remarks.

"Oh Shafi Mia," taunted Halima when she saw him in the marketplace, "Have you heard that Rabeya has a beautiful new goat the likes of which the village has never seen before? Any day now the goat will have kids which Rabeya will sell for so much money that, not only will she be able to buy the best seeds and fertilizer, but will also be able to hire labourers to farm their plot of land."

"Shafi Mia," the Imam said to him gravely, when he went to the mosque to pray, "Allah protects the poor. You who say your prayers five times a day, never miss a day of fasting during Ramadan, and every year pay for whitewashing the mosque, should not have tried to cheat Rabeya. After all Khalil is an invalid and they are so poor."

"Ah, Shafi Mia," said the village headman, barely being able to stifle his laughter. "I hear you are having trouble with goats and women. If you want peace inside and outside your home, you better settle the matter before your wife returns and finds out what has happened in her absence. You know how high she holds her nose because her brother is a politician in the next village."

Angry as he was, Shafi Mia realized that he had been outsmarted and stalemated by a group of poor women. Since everyone knew about the matter, it was too late to send his hired hands to forcibly bring back the animal. Besides, too much excitement in her delicate condition may be harmful for his precious goat. What he owed Rabeya was a fraction of what he had paid for the goat, and his withholding the money was more for forcing Rabeya and Khalil to sell the land, rather than for monetary benefit. So, much as he disliked it, Shafi Mia decided to pay Rabeya the full share of the profits.

That evening Shafi Mia's son delivered the money to Rabeya, who then allowed the boy to lead the goat home. Grateful to Allah for helping her and her friends win this round, she made a mental note to say a few extra verses of prayers in thanksgiving.

As she sliced the green and white striped marrow for the evening meal, Rabeya pondered on the nature of man. Shafi Mia had so much, yet he was not satisfied and wanted to take away from them even the little that Khalil and she owned. Why did the rich and powerful prey on the poor and the weak? Why did one always have to fight for one's rights when things could be so simple if everyone trusted and helped each other. Why was the world such an unfair place?

The stars shone down on Rabeya, and the embers glowed in the *chula*. Like the steam rising from the bubbling pot, her thoughts dissipated into the evening air to mingle with the same unanswered questions of centuries of philosophers and sages.